Dear Spencer

Dear Spencer

Love Notes SERIES

DANIELLE KEIL

ALSO BY
Danielle Keil

The Parkdale Series

The Pact Series

The Ainsworth Royals:
The Next Gen Series

Love Notes Series

To all the girls who feel overlooked for being the brains and not the beauty—this one is for you. Hold your head high and make those spreadsheets color coded. Your envelope is coming.

It felt weird to leave the house without a backpack. "Bye, Mom! See you in a few hours!" I grabbed my car keys off the hook, slipped my purse over my shoulder, and opened the door to the garage before she responded.

"Wait!" Mom rushed down the stairs, waving something in her hands. "This came for you yesterday. Dad put the mail on our dresser and I didn't notice it until now."

We both laughed. Dad had a knack for putting things in different places every time. Pots and pans never had a steady home, and Mom banned him from unloading the dishwasher ever again.

"Aw, look at you. Your last day of junior year. First official day as student body president," Mom gushed, placing a hand over her chest, her eyes slightly watering.

I sighed. No matter what I did in life, Mom would be proud of me. She told everyone she met about my straight

A's, my honor roll status, being class president, and now, student body president.

"What is that?" I asked, gesturing to what was in her hand. I froze when she lifted it and extend it toward me.

"Where did you get that?" I spat out in a harsher tone than I meant to.

The smile on her face stretched ear to ear. The two of us were identical in most every way; from our naturally wavy brown hair to bright green eyes, I was my mother's daughter.

"I knew what it was the second I saw it. Do you have time to open it?" she whispered, as if it was all a secret. No one else was home, so I wasn't sure who she was keeping it down for.

"No," I mumbled, reaching once again for the door. "I will when I get home."

We only had about three hours of school today, being the last official day and all. Summer break started in exactly four hours.

Mom's face fell. "Well, alright honey. Enjoy your last day."

I turned and gave her a hug. After slipping into the car that used to be my father's, I took off toward school, the piece of mail still on my mind.

As I drove, I racked my brain. I had never heard of a teal envelope being mailed before. It looked weird with a stamp and postage on it. And they wrote my name smaller than normal, to accommodate for my address as well.

I paused as I pulled into the parking lot. To my left was student parking. To the right was faculty. Usually, I went in the second row of student parking.

But today was my first day as acting student body president. The seniors normally ditched the last day, making the juniors official seniors. We all wore our new black senior shirts and shorts, claiming our stakes on the next school year.

But... did that mean I could park in the student body president spot? It was the first one in the front row. Prime parking real estate.

Considering it was empty, I turned toward it, my palms sweaty on the wheel. Now that it was right in front of me, the entire job seemed overwhelming.

A horn honked behind my car, startling me. I waved an apology and inched my way into the spot. It felt wrong, but I knew it wasn't. Convincing my brain of that was hard, though.

"Wow, look at you, Madam President!" someone called as soon as I opened my door. Fixing my tortoiseshell glasses on my nose, I looked up, finding Skye with a hand on her hip, staring me down.

I rolled my eyes. "I don't even know if I'm supposed to park here."

Skye matched my rolled eyes and stumbled toward me, pulling me into a hug. She loved hugs. Me, not so much, but I put up with it. No one could say no to Skye; she was just too nice.

"Well, Madam President, what's the first task for today?"

I reached in and grabbed my purse. "No tasks. Just going to enjoy the last day."

Skye giggled as we walked toward school. "Do you feel different? We're seniors now, Spence. Seniors!"

3

"Technically, we're still juniors. We have to survive the summer first." I stopped short of the front doors. Why this moment felt monumental, I wasn't certain. But like Skye said, something was different.

"Right?" Skye asked, nudging me in the shoulder. "I feel it too."

But Skye didn't know what awaited me at home. She didn't realize that today was June second, which meant the secret admirers chose a new girl yesterday.

"Secret Admirers?" she asked as I opened the front door.

I blinked, staring at her. This habit of mumbling under my breath got me in trouble sometimes.

"Um, yeah. I mean, it's June second. Shouldn't someone have been chosen yesterday?" I tried to brush it off as if I was just curious, not that I had any actual information on it.

Skye shrugged. "Not sure. Sometimes they don't play in the summer, remember?"

"Yeah," I nodded, adjusting the strap of my purse. "That's right."

"I didn't hear about a teal envelope being on anyone's locker yesterday, either. So maybe it's an off month."

I sucked in a breath and held it an extra beat, watching everyone around us laugh and greet their friends. Today was a formality. A few hours in school to fulfill the necessary time for the state. We already cleared out our lockers and there was no work to be done. Hence the reason no one had a backpack.

"Will I see you after Transfer?" I asked Skye, as I turned toward the courtyard.

"Well, we won't be here for lunch. But we'll definitely get together before I leave, right?"

Pausing, I turned back and threw myself at her in a huge hug. "Gah, I'm so sorry! I'm a bit distracted today. When do you leave on your trip?"

Skye and her family were doing a full itinerary through Europe this summer. They would be gone for four weeks, gallivanting from country to country.

I wasn't jealous. Not one bit. That's the lie I've been telling myself for a while now, anyway.

"Next week. I still haven't packed a single thing."

She laughed when my eyes widened in fear. Had it been me, I would have had a list of items to pack three weeks ago, had all my shopping done, and the suitcases taken out. Laundry would be done at the end of this week and the packing would be finalized two days before. Right on schedule.

Skye started down the hallway, but yelled over her shoulder, "I'll text you before we go! Let's grab coffee!"

I waved, my heart still pounding from the second-hand anxiety she caused. Normally, I would head straight to my locker before class, but today I hit the courtyard first.

Traditions at Ryder High were important to us. Besides the Secret Admirers, the Transfer between juniors and seniors was a ritual not to be missed.

I wanted to be the first to arrive, to greet my fellow classmates as we huddled in the corridor next to the courtyard doors. But I wasn't first.

Marcus Edmond was, sitting on a bench, sipping out of a reusable coffee cup. He had one ankle resting on his other knee, khaki shorts, and a collared polo with the top two buttons undone.

"Prez," he said as I approached, tilting his head down and lifting his cup in a cheers gesture. "Take a seat?"

I narrowed my eyes at him, trying to figure out his motive. Marcus never did anything without a motive.

"Mr. Senior Class President, how are you the first one here?" The announcement of his new title brought a smile to his face.

Marcus and I flip-flopped class president over the years. I won freshman year, then he overtook me sophomore year. This year, I claimed the title again, and most recently we battled it out for student body president.

Which I won. And as a consolation prize, he got to be senior class president. Which meant we would work side by side. All year.

"Coffee from Sips was fresh, the line was short, and beating you to something is always a pleasure," he replied with a wink.

Was Marcus Edmond cocky? Yes. Was he a jerk? Sometimes. Did he know exactly how to get under my skin? Every freaking day.

Was he also one of the smartest guys in our class? Yes. Did he do a good job as president? Reluctantly, yes.

I sighed and crossed my arms. "Whatever. The least you could have done was bring—"

"You a coffee? How about an extra hot, salted caramel, dark chocolate mocha, no whip?" he interrupted, reaching behind his back and pulling out another cup.

My jaw dropped. My lips flapped like a fish out of water. The one redeeming quality that Marcus had was his brain. He remembered every little detail about everything he ever went through. Or so it seemed most days.

Like right now—my perfect coffee order. How he remembered, I wasn't sure, but there he sat, arm outreached, waiting for me to take the cup.

I did and perched on the edge of the bench two feet away from him. "Thank you," I mumbled, not forgetting my manners.

He uncrossed his legs and leaned his elbows on his knees, holding his cup with both hands as he looked at me. "Notice anything?" he asked.

In fact, I had noticed. The second I walked up, I noticed.

But complimenting Marcus usually left a bad taste in my mouth, so I held back.

"I finally found contacts that don't make my eyes react and blow up twice their size," he said with a grin. He fluttered his lashes before bursting out laughing.

"Well, at least before, your swollen eyes would match your swollen head and massive ego," I muttered, both hoping he heard me and not.

He did. And he let out a roar, slapping his knee. "That was good, Spence." The serious look returned half a second later.

"Now, as senior class president, I believe it is my duty to lead the huddle and the dash, correct?"

I froze. I should have known better. The motive. Everything until now was an act, including buying me my favorite coffee and making small talk. He was waiting to drop this bomb on me.

The harsh reality was that he was right. In the back of my mind, I expected it. It was the reason I tried to get here before anyone else, to affirm my position.

But, I failed. "Well, I think—"

Marcus held up a hand. "Nope. Tradition clearly states that the new senior class president presides over the festivities. Not the student body president. Not the outgoing junior class president. Senior class. Me."

He didn't even try to hide his smug little smirk. I wanted to dump the coffee over his head. "Fine," I said through gritted teeth.

I would finish my coffee, and I would like it, if only to spite him. The coffee didn't do anything to deserve my rage; he did.

It took another ten minutes before the rest of the upcoming senior class arrived, all in our black shirts. Some had black face paint in streaks on their cheeks, or our graduating year written on their faces.

"Seniors!" Marcus bellowed as he climbed up onto the bench, cupping his hands around his mouth. "It is time. It is *our* time!"

The crowd in front of him thundered in return, clapping, shouting, stomping of feet. Ryder High was one of the smaller schools in the district, with only about two hundred students per class, but at that moment, it felt like we could fill an entire arena.

I sucked in a breath and held it, trying to push down the negative thoughts creeping in. The ones that said I should have been up there leading our friends. That everyone was going to look at me and laugh, thinking I was a failure.

"Are you ready?" Marcus yelled. The crowd hollered. "Then let's GO!"

Marcus jumped down from the bench and started down the path cleared for him, allowing him to be the first through the doors of the courtyard.

But then he did something unthinkable. Something that made everyone pause, including myself. He turned, took a few steps back, and grabbed my hand, pulling me to the front with him.

"Together?" he asked with a smile that I couldn't find a single speck of mockery in. I swallowed my pride and nodded.

Side by side, a place I never usually liked being with Marcus Edmond, we pushed through the doors and jogged into the massive courtyard.

The lower grades were waiting, along with numerous teachers, front office staff, and the principal standing in the middle.

The new junior class and sophomore class presidents stood a few feet away, holding a paper banner with "juniors" written across it. Marcus and I upped our speed, careening into the banner and ripping it apart.

As we got to the middle of the courtyard, another banner appeared, held by Principal Salgoa. He gave it to Marcus first, who then handed me one side. We both jumped on the closest bench and held it over our heads as our classmates filled in the space in front of us.

Seniors, the new banner read.

I looked around, finding my friends in the crowd. Skye, with her bright blonde hair making her easy to spot, next to a new girl this year, McKinnon. Emilia and Mya, side by side with Chase and Tucker and the rest of our study group.

Marcus started chanting, "Seniors, seniors, seniors," as a wave of something came over me. I couldn't quite place the feeling, but it made me feel empowered, confident, and happy.

The jocks to the right of me — the baseball boys, the football team, and even the soccer players — began to get a bit rowdy, but that was alright. It was our moment.

It was our year.

At least, it would be. After we had the best dang summer yet.

"I'm home!" I hollered as soon as I dropped my purse on the kitchen counter and kicked my sandals off in the direction of the shoe rack. A drink and a snack were necessary before I had enough energy to put them away. Probably a real lunch, or I would become hangry, but a snack was all I had stamina for.

After the Transfer, Principal Salgoa made everyone go to their homeroom, much to the chagrin of every student. Except me.

He held me back, wanting to discuss plans for the presidents. Every summer, we held meetings at least once a month in order to have everything ready for the school year. They were voluntary, as it was summer and the school couldn't mandate anything on breaks, but I had never missed one. Even the year Marcus was president, I still attended. If anything happened to Marcus, the role automatically shifted to me, so I had to be up to date.

No one else ever saw it that way, but Principal Salgoa appreciated my attendance regardless.

Today, he kept me for a full thirty minutes before calling in the other class presidents. We went over the schedule for the summer, what would be discussed, and what each president needed to get done before school resumed in August. My job was to make sure they all stayed on task, covered the Homecoming committee needs, and spoke with our local business liaisons for fundraising efforts in the fall.

"How'd it go, sweetheart? How was Transfer?" Mom asked as she waltzed into the kitchen with a grin on her face.

I slumped onto a stool at the island and dropped my head into my arms. "It was great," I mumbled.

"Did you get the planning done?" Mom was always current on what was happening in my life. It was a mixture of curiosity and me spending a lot of time rambling about my projects and work.

I reached an arm out across the counter, with my palm up, and beckoned her with my fingers. In a moment, an apple landed in my hand.

Lifting my head, I took three big bites of before I answered her. While I ate, she started on some dishes.

"Planning done. Schedule made. Everything is organized and set up. I hope the sophomore class president does her job, though. She seems a little..." I paused, trying to think of the word. Juniper was sweet, but she didn't always bring her whole brain with her.

"A little not like you?" Mom offered with a knowing smile.

I sighed. Really, I wasn't as superficial as people sometimes thought. I gave everyone a chance. But if you blew that chance... then yes, I may judge you a bit differently.

"Well, she'll get some good counsel from you this year, that I'm sure," Mom said, drying her hands on a dish towel and turning toward me.

After I finished my apple, I told Mom I was going upstairs to rest. The day hadn't been particularly exhausting, but there was something up there I needed to look at.

The second I entered my room, I looked over at my desk. Mom put the envelope there, as well as a stack of laundry, waiting for me.

Ignoring the laundry, I sat in my chair and reached for the envelope. I had seen many of them over the past few years, even helping some girls figure out their own Secret Admirer.

But never did I think *I* would get one. I was Spencer Matthews. Super nerd, overly organized, and determined to make a name for myself in this world.

It wasn't that I had never had a boyfriend before. I did, sophomore year. Tucker and I lasted a whopping three months before we decided to just be friends and nothing more.

I was too goal oriented, he said. Not in a bad way, just in the way that dividing my attention between things was difficult. When I made something a priority, I put my all into it. And unfortunately, our little flirt with dating came as I was running for junior class president toward the end of sophomore year. I couldn't focus on both him and the election, and ultimately, our relationship suffered.

It was for the best, though. I loved Tucker as a friend, a study buddy, and a helpful hand when I needed posters created for elections. He was on the set crew for theater, and his artistic skills were out of this world amazing.

But with my goals for the future, a boyfriend wasn't in my cards.

Which made the teal envelope in front of me even more confusing. Everyone knew me. I wasn't the most popular person, but I made it my mission to get to know at least the names of everyone in our graduating class. I couldn't very well ask for their votes if I didn't know them and they didn't know me, right?

With hesitation, I grabbed my letter opener from the pencil cup next to my laptop and slid it under the flap, keeping the envelope mostly intact.

Girls all across my grade revered the teal envelope. They thought it held some sort of magic powers and granted all your life's wishes if you got one.

I wasn't quite that obsessed with the game, but I enjoyed it. It was fun and allowed guys who may be too shy a chance at finding their perfect match too.

Holding my breath, I slid out the pale lavender paper and read.

Spencer–

The men of Ryder High invite you to become part of an exclusive club of exquisite people like yourself. Ones who are admired and revered, but from afar.

Dear Spencer

Acceptance of this invitation will start your month-long journey into finding out who sent you this letter. The man who craves your attention, yet strays from your spotlight. He may be someone you know, or someone you have never met.

But he knows you. And he chose you. In the end, it is his wish to be with you in whatever context you prefer. It's all up to you. Nothing during this month is mandatory. You can stop at any time. If you are ever uncomfortable, a neutral party can be spoken with, and alternatives can be made.

<u>*You are in control.*</u>

The secret admirers are chosen and vetted. There is no mal-intent involved with this invitation. You may choose to decline the invitation all together without any backlash. You have our guarantee that no harm will come to you in any form.

If you wish for more information regarding the history of the secret admirers, please text the number at the bottom. All your questions, within reason and without ruining the mystery, will be answered to the best of our ability.

For now, the first question is for you.

Do you accept?

Sincerely—
Your Secret Admirer

I read the paper three times, even though I already had it memorized. It was the same initial invitation that every chosen girl got on the first of the month.

If the girl, meaning me, didn't respond, the game went on as planned. If she wanted to get out, she had to call or text the number.

No one at Ryder knew who was behind the number. The "neutral party" had to be random and unbiased. They were the ones that chose the boys each month and put the whole shebang together. It obviously changed each year, with graduating seniors and all.

I never gave it too much thought, as I had other things to worry about. Mainly, figuring out who my secret admirer was. Considering I knew everyone, it couldn't be that hard, right? As long as he followed the rules and gave me the clues I needed without being vague about it.

I placed the note down on the desk and tilted my head up to the bookshelf that sat above me. After thinking for a moment, I pulled down a brand-new blue notebook. Blue seemed like the perfect color to use for this project.

ot five minutes into my preparation, my phone buzzed. Sighing, I lowered the green pen I was using to outline a box for potential secret admirers, and picked up the phone.

> **UNKNOWN:** It starts tomorrow. Keep your phone close.

My brows furrowed. I wanted to respond, but I thought it through first. An unknown number, sending a message the day after the teal envelope arrived. The day that the game was supposed to start.

Thinking about it, I sort of unintentionally accepted. I was going to anyway, but since Mom didn't give me the letter when it actually arrived, and silence was acceptance, then my Secret Admirer had no idea I didn't technically accept until now.

"What a horrible plan," I said to myself, picking up my pen and tapping it against my lips. "They should have done it the other way around. You have to call or text the number and let them know you're a willing participant. What if someone didn't see the letter right away? What if they forgot or fell asleep or didn't get around to messaging? It's quite backwards..."

Deciding that the message was ultimately a part of the game, I ignored it. I would keep my phone by me, but I first wanted to finish the outline for my plans so I could transfer them to my computer and make a real color-coded spreadsheet. This was just the rough draft.

Once I finished, I bounded downstairs to help Mom with dinner. I spent the entire afternoon in my room organizing, and I felt refreshed and ready to go.

"What time is Dad coming home? I have some last-minute questions to ask him about tomorrow," I asked Mom as I set the table.

Tomorrow started my first day as an unpaid, but eager, intern at Dad's law office. Mainly, I would be the grunt—the coffee-getter, paper-shredder, garbage collecting nobody. But I was excited to be in on the action, and Dad promised I could sit in and take notes on some meetings when appropriate.

It was a part-time thing, only two days a week for half a day each, but at only seventeen, it was an amazing start and perfect for my resume. Elle Woods, eat your heart out.

"He should be here right as dinner gets—" Mom started, but the opening of the door to the garage cut her off. "Or now. Now is good too. Hi, sweetie," she whispered, standing on her tip-toes to give him a kiss.

Coming in a few inches over six feet, Dad was a giant. I got the height gene from him, as I was a whopping five foot ten inches tall. I towered over a few of the boys at school, minus most of the jocks.

"What's cookin', good lookin'," he said to Mom after balancing his briefcase on the shoe rack by the back door. She giggled and swatted at his butt with the pot holder before returning to the oven.

"Were you ladies talking about me?" Dad grabbed a glass of water and turned his attention toward me.

"I was. I want to go over a few details about tomorrow." I leaned against the counter, waiting for directions from Mom.

Dad and I delved into a lengthy conversation that traversed into the dining room and through the meal. Mom kept to herself, popping in now and then when she had an opinion. But when Dad and I got started, it was hard to stop us.

"Goodnight, Spence. You'll do great tomorrow," Dad said after we cleaned up and I headed to the shower. He ruffled my hair, just like he used to when I was little.

Tomorrow was a big day for me, and I couldn't wait. I went to bed, completely forgetting what else tomorrow had in store...

"Nancy, your grande caramel latte, non-fat, no whip. James, your venti black, no sugar, no cream, no 'floofy crap'," I said with a wink, placing each cup in front of the people around the table.

"Ha!" James barked, grabbing the cup and raising it toward my father. "You've taught her well, Matthews."

Considering I had known James since I was three, I just shook my head and continued passing out coffee orders. Dad was going to let me sit in on this meeting, as it didn't pertain to any specific case, and therefore had no confidential information was being discussed.

When I offered to go downstairs and fulfill the needs for afternoon caffeine uptakes before the meeting, they all looked at me as some sort of god. And I took it.

I settled myself into the chair in the corner, away from the table, my legal pad of paper balanced on my thighs. My pencil skirt came to just below my knee with a small slit in the back. I unbuttoned the button on my matching black blazer before I sat.

My tortoiseshell glasses nestled on my nose, and I was ready for action.

The second Dad opened his mouth to begin the meeting, my phone jingled. Not buzzed, jingled. Full on noise and sound.

My cheeks burst into flames as I dug into my blazer pocket. "I'm so sorry. I always have this thing on silent, but I put it on to hear it in the coffee shop in case of an extra order, and—"

"Just turn it off, Spence," Dad said, stopping my rant.

"Yes, sir," I replied, biting my lip and staring down at my black two-inch pumps. I bought them specifically for today. But now it seemed like a dumb move.

I embarrassed myself right after I had made a great first impression. This is what everyone around the table would remember about today, not the good deed with the coffee.

After shutting the phone completely off to ensure there would be no more interruptions, I shoved it back into my pocket and lifted my pen again.

The rest of the afternoon went by without incident. I followed directions, made copies, and delivered folders to offices when needed.

I didn't speak on the car ride home. Dad, sensing my need for silence, turned on the radio softly instead, humming along to songs he recognized.

"I'm going to shower. I'll grab a snack later, if that's alright. I'm not super hungry," I asked Mom as we came into the kitchen.

She glanced at Dad, who nodded. "That's fine, honey. I made some homemade chicken fingers and threw a salad together. I'll make you a plate and pop it into the fridge for whenever you're ready."

After thanking her and giving Dad a smile, I bounded up the stairs two at a time. I couldn't wait to get out of this outfit, drench myself in the hottest water possible, and jump into my sweats.

I cycled through my calming mantras during the scalding shower. The hotter, the better to wash away my worries with. A mixture of deep breaths, repeating words, and lavender-mint body wash left me a new person by the time the water got cold.

Next came a thorough skin care routine. Once that was finished, I had no motivation to do anything with my hair besides wrap it up in a microfiber towel and pin it tight.

Flopping on my bed, my first instinct was to scroll through social media for a while and zone out before picking a movie on a streaming service before falling asleep.

But the moment I picked up my phone, I remembered what happened in the meeting room. It didn't faze me as much as it would have an hour ago, since my mantras were that good, but seeing the phone still off threw me for a loop. It had been off for hours by this point, and who knew how many messages I had missed.

I held my breath as the phone started up, anticipating the massive amount of pings and jingles alerting me to everything that happened since earlier this afternoon.

To my surprise, there were only two missed text messages. I scrolled through, answering one, and chuckling at the meme Emilia sent, but not sending a response of my own.

Letting out a long breath, I relaxed into my pillows, a weight lifted off my shoulder. I hated the feeling of being out of touch and reveled when I realized there had been no fires set in my absence.

Had this been during the school year and not in the summer, things would have been worse. Someone always needed something, or things had to be taken care of. But during the summer, I could relax a bit more.

I didn't get comfortable, however, as I bolted upright, remembering that something else set my phone off during the meeting.

was supposed to keep my phone close by. The text from yesterday, from my secret admirer, said so.

Scrolling through notifications for half a second led me to it—some odd message with a link.

Normally, I ignored things like that and blocked them as fast as possible. But... I was told I would have a message today. Was this it?

Hesitantly, I messaged back, just in case. I didn't dare to click the link in case it was spam and a virus. I knew better than that.

ME: Is this real? Not a spam link?

UNKNOWN: Yes, this is what your secret admirer would like you to click. It is not spam, and will lead you to further directions.

I hovered my finger over the link, still a bit unsure. Most secret admirers just sent clues in more letters or something. Why did mine send a link? What did it lead to?

"Only one way to find out," I whispered and lowered my finger, allowing a new window to open.

An app. I was supposed to download a new app.

I pressed download and waited. What was this? And what did the title mean, trivia for a clue?

The first thing in my mind was the fact that whoever this guy was, he must know me well enough to know how much I love random trivia. Trivia games, trivia shows, movie trivia, music, celebrities, books, you name it, I know it. It was a skill Dad and I also shared—stowing away miscellaneous bits and pieces at all times.

I reached over and jotted down a note on the sticky notepad on my nightstand before opening the app.

> *Congratulations, Spencer! You have begun
> your journey into finding out who is behind this
> game. You have cleared the first task and can
> now begin.*

A flashing red button saying "Begin" beckoned me, so I clicked it. A shower of confetti filled my screen before falling out of the frame, leaving me with text being typed on a piece of notebook paper.

> *Your clues for this game will come via this app. Every time it is updated, it will alert you. Now, I wouldn't be your secret admirer without knowing a bit about you and your competitive streak. Therefore, I created this app to make you work for your clues.*

The typing stopped, and the notebook paper got ripped away, a fresh piece replacing it.

> *Each time you log in, you will play a game to get your clue. Trivia is the game of choice. Answer 3 of 5 questions correct to obtain the random clue to my identity. Get less than 3, and you'll have to wait 12-24 hours to try again.*

My heart jumped. The one thing I hated in life was failure, and having to wait to correct my mistakes came in a close second. My secret admirer seemed to know my faults and my strengths.

> *Your first game begins now. Good luck!*

More confetti fell, taking the papers with it. "Begin" flashed in front of me again. I clicked it fast.

A game show type board came on the screen with the numbers one through 5 lit up on the left-hand side. A box popped up above it with a question.

Who painted the Mona Lisa?

I laughed. That was too easy. I clicked on da Vinci. The name went straight to the line next to number one, and another box appeared.

What does SUV stand for?

Another easy one. If they were all going to be like this, it would be a piece of cake. Sport Utility Vehicle appeared next to the number two, and I continued on.

Tercel is the name for a male of what type of animal?

This one gave me pause. The options were mongoose, hawk, anteater, or armadillo. I eliminated mongoose and anteater right away from instinct. But armadillo or mongoose... I couldn't decide and would have to risk it. I couldn't click out of the app to check either. Not only would it be cheating, but I didn't want to lose my place and risk starting over. Or worse, having to wait if it counted it as a failure.

I went with the hawk, and cheered out loud when I saw it jump next to the number three. I already won this round, but it seemed like I had to answer all five just in case.

What is a group of witches called?

Dear Spencer

Simple—a coven. After it filled in next to number four, the last question appeared on the screen.

Who was Germany's first female chancellor?

I didn't even need the options for that one. Glancing up, I saw her picture on my women leader's poster board above my desk. Angela Merkel filled in the last remaining line and the confetti was back.

I congratulated myself as a message of the same came on the screen.

"Your Clue" button appeared, and I smashed it with more enthusiasm than I had the buttons earlier.

The notebook paper was back.

Great job! I had no doubts you would pass the first day. Don't worry, they'll get harder each time. I know I don't have to say this to you, but no cheating! If you are with other people at the time you play, I'll allow helpful hints. But no Google or searching the internet or books for the answer. I still have control over the app and can put a timer in place if needed.

Your clue for today is:

Closer than you may think, yet so far away. In the shadows I've always been, but now I'm ready to play.

Until next time,
Your secret admirer

After the text finished, even more confetti fell, until it returned to the home screen, just the title of the app appearing.

I exited out, wondering what in the world it could all mean. Before I forgot, I wrote down the clue word for word.

Tomorrow, I would have to begin analyzing.

After I hit the beach with the girls, of course.

Chapter 6

"Can someone get my back before I flip over?" Skye asked, reaching her arm out to the side, sunscreen in hand, to anyone that would answer. Her oversized shades and floppy hat covered her face like a shield.

"I got you," I answered, sitting up and taking the bottle from her. Upon further inspection, I deemed it perfect for my fair skin as well. "Do mine after?"

Skye nodded, pulled her hair away from her shoulders, and turned around. I slathered the lotion on her back, rubbing the excess into my arms before spinning around myself.

"So, what is everyone up to this summer?" Emilia asked. She was covered head to toe and under the giant umbrella in the shade. With her red hair and masses of freckles, she didn't take any chances in the sun.

"Thanks," I muttered to Skye as she finished my back. We both turned and laid on our stomachs on our towels, covering our faces with our hats. "I'm working part time at my dad's law office. Grunt work, but it'll look good on college applications. And then president stuff, of course."

"Of course, presidential duties. Your summer break consisted of a whopping, what, two days?" Emilia chided, with a smile on her face.

I tried to reach out and swat at her, but she was too far away for me. I was in the middle, with Skye to my right and Emilia to my left. She sat in a beach chair instead of a lounger, reading a book I hadn't heard of. She was big into indie authors she found through social media.

"Better to be prepared before the school year starts than to come back to a dumpster fire," I responded, leaning over to take a sip from my water bottle. We had only been here an hour, but it was almost empty. The beach wasn't super crowded; the season had barely begun, and while the sun felt warm, the temperature didn't hit above 85 yet. Once it hit a consistent 90, it would be hard to get a spot to lay out.

Emilia turned back to her book, and I was pretty sure Skye was almost asleep. I made a mental note to wake her when I flipped over so she didn't burn.

A few quiet minutes later, my phone chirped. I kept it on, as Mom was going to call when she needed me home to go bring Grandma the frozen dinners she made for her this week. I never passed up a chance to meet with Grandma—she was one of my biggest role models and one of the most badass women of her time. Even to this day, she wouldn't hesitate to cuss you out and put you in your place if you were in her way.

I ignored the buzz at first, wanting to keep my eyes

closed a minute longer. Since I knew it was Mom, I didn't bother looking.

"What's 'Trivia for a Clue'?" Skye asked. I jerked to the side, almost falling out of the lounger. I assumed she was asleep, so to hear her voice startled me.

"What?" I gasped, swinging my legs over and planting my feet in the sand. I glanced down to make sure my bikini hadn't shifted, then stared at Skye. She was a bit fuzzy, since my glasses were in my bag.

She pointed to my phone, which somehow was closer to her than me, and face up. The notification from the alert sat on the screen. I grabbed my glasses and slid them on to see what it said.

Trivia for a Clue sent you a message: New Entry

My cheeks flushed as I snatched the phone away, holding it close to my chest. "Nothing. It's nothing."

A sly grin came on upon Skye's face. "Uh huh. And my gran is the Queen of England. Fess up, girlfriend."

I narrowed my eyes at her. "You say that phrase a lot. Aren't there any other unreasonable expressions you can think of?"

She huffed out a little laugh and sat up in her own chair. Emilia caught wind of our discussion and jumped over my chair to join Skye, the both of them staring me down.

"What?" I tried to act innocent. "It's just an app."

"A clue? Like a... I don't know... secret admirer clue?" Emilia said, her grin matching Skye's. She took off her hat and fluffed her ringlets, scratching at her scalp before replacing the hat on her head.

"Excuse *moi*, but did you get chosen as the 'it girl' for June? I didn't think they chose anyone this month, because it's summer!"

Lying was not my specialty. Everyone said so. I couldn't even hold in a little white lie. If I had to withhold information from someone for any reason, I took the avoidance route.

It didn't take long for me to break down. "Ugh, *fine*. Yes. It's me. I was chosen."

A pause. A few blinks. Then, Skye turned to Emilia, the two of them joined hands, and squealed. Loud.

After covering my ears with my hands, I shushed them. "Guys! Stop! What are you doing?"

"Oh my gosh, Spence, this is so cool! I haven't known anyone to get chosen yet! Not like, personally anyway!" Emilia gushed.

I sighed. "Well, pretend you didn't hear me say that, alright? Let's just forget this happened and go back to laying out."

My suggestion fell flat, as I assumed it would.

"Oh, heck no! Tells us *everything*," Skye started, leaning forward and placing her elbows on her knees and her chin in her hands.

There was no way out of this. Neither one of my friends would let me leave this beach until they had all the info.

Rolling my eyes, I responded, "Fine. He mailed the initial teal envelope on the first. Mom didn't see it until the morning of the second, so by default, I agreed to enter to play without even knowing I was chosen."

Emilia nodded slowly, her lips in a tight line as she gathered the details.

"Then I got a text with a link to download this app." I pulled my phone away from my chest and showed them the notification. "It's some sort of trivia app. I have to answer five questions, and get three of them right, to get a clue."

Skye's brows shot up. "Wow. Okay, so it's definitely someone who knows you. Because if someone tried to pull that with *me*, I would be out on the first day." She laughed, which allowed us to laugh with her. Skye was a smart girl, but more of a street-smart person than book smarts.

"So, the notification just now means..." Emilia started.

"There's a new round to play."

The three of us huddled in the back of my old Jeep Cherokee, our stuff pushed against the seats so we could sit with our legs dangling.

"Why am I nervous? This isn't even my game," Skye whispered. "And why am I whispering? It's not like anyone is here or knows what we're doing!"

Emilia managed a little giggle, but I stayed silent as I swiped across my phone and opened the app.

Welcome to Level 2

The box on the screen was the same as yesterday. The next button said 'Begin', just like last time. I clicked in, waiting for the notebook paper to give me a message, but it went straight into the questions, with the game show board in the background.

What is the chemical symbol for lead?

"Whaaaaa?" Skye muttered. Thankfully, we had options to choose from, because even I didn't know that one off the top of my head.

"Oh, it's Pb," said Emilia, pointing to the option on the screen. Considering she was on track to be valedictorian, I didn't question her and pressed the answer. It flew back onto the board next to the number one.

Grand Teton National Park is located in what state?

"Oh, I got that one! Wyoming! We went there on our cross-country road trip last summer," Skye exclaimed. I pressed it, and it jumped on the board.

"Yes! Score one for Skye!" she said with a fist pump.

Who was assassinated by Nathuram Godse?

"Ha. He thought he could stump me, but little does he know I did an entire project on Gandhi freshman year," I huffed, a wave of confidence coming over me.

"Or maybe he did know..." Emilia hinted, knocking her shoulder into mine.

My smile dropped. Did he? I did the project as extra-credit for Geography; it wasn't an assigned piece of work.

"So... is that it? That's three, right?" Skye asked before I locked in the answer.

"No, we have to go through all five either way," I answered, then put Gandhi on the board.

What chess piece makes an L-shaped move?

I didn't even read the answers before looking straight at Emilia to my right. Skye leaned around me and did the same. She was the president of the chess club, so we didn't even try to answer ourselves.

"The knight," she answered confidently. Skye and I grinned at her.

"Last one," I whispered before sending it to the final question.

How many symphonies did Beethoven compose?

I froze. My random knowledge did not include this piece of information. A quick look to my friends confirmed they were as clueless as I.

"Well... we already got the three needed to get to the clue. It doesn't matter if we get this one wrong." I tried to convince them, but it was myself who needed convincing. I hated being wrong.

"Skye, why don't you take a random guess?" I tilted the phone so she could see the options more clearly.

She let out a large breath, puffing out her cheeks. "Ummmm..." she drew out, staring at the screen as if her grade depended on it. "I'll go with seven."

I clicked it, and a red X appeared over the text.

Incorrect. The correct answer is: 9.

The confetti returned this time, much to Skye's delight.

"We won!" she squealed, squeezing me from the side.

A message of congratulations filled the screen, and the button to take me to the clue appeared.

The text scrolled on the notebook paper, just like it had previously.

> *Nice work! I hope you're enjoying the game. The questions have been fun for me to find, and it's my goal to make them challenging enough for you as well. The last thing I would want is for you to be bored with this game. I may not be like some of the recent Secret Admirers, but I like to think I know how to have fun.*
>
> *Your clue for today is:*
> *More flip-flops than a beach in summer.*
> *Enjoy your summer, Spencer.*
>
> *Your Secret Admirer*

"What? Does he know we're at the beach right now?" Skye cried, looking around.

"No..." I muttered. There was no way he could. He had to have uploaded this prior, with specific directions to which message to play if I passed or failed.

"What does he mean, flip-flops? And more than a beach in summer? That's a lot," Emilia piped in.

"Did you get a clue yesterday?" Skye asked, suddenly interested in me again instead of the beach goers.

"Something about a shadow? I wrote it down at home. I can't remember."

Emilia pointed at the screen. "What if you press that? Does it take you to any sort of menu?"

I felt embarrassed that I hadn't thought of that. I tapped on the three lines, and sure enough, a menu popped up.

"There, that one," she said, gesturing to the link that said 'Previous Clues'.

"Close, but far. Shadows, and now play? How is that even a clue?" Skye asked.

"Put it together with flip-flops... I can't think of anything, sorry." Emilia shrugged. "I'd have to think about this, but another clue seems needed."

I nodded and slipped my phone into my pocket after I jumped out of the trunk. "Hey, I gotta get going. Mom is taking dinner to Grandma, and I told her I'd tag along."

Emilia and Skye scrambled out of my car. Em drove the two of them, so we said our goodbyes.

The entire drive home I thought about flip flops, beaches, and shadows. None of it made a lick of sense, but the view of the spreadsheet jumped into my mind. I mentally began to fill it in with possibilities and reasoning.

I couldn't wait to get to my laptop and do it for real. Emilia may not have been able to come up with anyone, but I sure had some ideas.

waited until the next morning to open my laptop and start inputting data. Mom and I ended up staying at Grandma's through dinner and way later than either of us realized. That, plus the time in the sun, left me utterly exhausted to the point where I forgot about the clues and went straight to sleep.

But now, after a quick shower to scrub off old sunscreen and sweat, I threw my hair into a bun, cleaned my glasses, and got to work.

The first thing I did was make sure my columns were all perfectly sized and ready for information. There were four so far—name, likely factor, clue number, and reasoning.

Each name I thought about would go on the list, no matter how big or small. Next, I would assign a number on how likely I thought that person would be my secret admirer, from one to five. Allotting a five meant that person was on the top of the list, and a one meant it was highly unlikely, but had to be put on the list for statistical purposes.

Clue number referred to which specific clue made me add the person. The more clues they related to, the higher the likeliness. And lastly, the reasoning. That line was purely subjective and based on my own opinion, but necessary just the same.

Each column was color coded, and I plugged in an equation—when the clue number column increased, the likelihood column increased. If someone linked to more than one clue, the likelihood increased by one each time.

By the time I finished creating the spreadsheet outline, my stomach rumbled. I didn't want to lose my motivation though, so I opted for a sip of my water bottle and a granola bar I kept in my desk drawer for late night study sessions. When that didn't satisfy me, I leaned down and opened the mini fridge Dad installed last year.

Grabbing a pre-made iced coffee and an apple, I got back to work. It would have to hold me over until I had the initial lists inputted.

I had to start at the beginning. Who knew I loved random trivia? I bit my cheek, thinking hard about when I used tidbits like that in my life.

Community Fundraiser Night. As class president, I got to run our night of community fundraiser for school. Once a year, the student body president chooses a charity or a good cause to fundraise for. We set aside a full week of activities to do to raise money, with each class getting a night to do something of their choosing. It cumulates on Friday with an all-out bash for students and the public.

Freshman year, I chose to run a trivia night. We sold tickets and everyone gathered in teams in the gym. I got to be the host and made the list of trivia questions myself.

Tapping my pen to my lips, I thought about who was on that committee with me.

As soon as names popped into my head, I typed them into the Name column.

Josh Nichols, Max Newman, Tucker Moore, and Marcus Edmond.

Tilting my head, I stared at the four names. Josh was a high possibility. I wasn't sure why, but I felt it in my gut. Max I was almost certain didn't fit. Tucker... well, there was history there, so maybe it could be him? Seemed unlikely, but I kept him as an option. And Marcus? Absolutely not. I didn't bother putting info in the other columns yet, as I still had more names to think of.

Next, I had to figure out who would be smart enough to build an app like the trivia game. Coding was a skill I never mastered, but there were a few names I could add to those above.

Chase McNeill and Jeremy Edwards were probably the two most computer savvy people I knew. It didn't seem like enough though, so I reached up and grabbed this year's yearbook off my bookshelf, flipping to the computer club photo.

Realistically, any of them could have made the app. But the Secret Admirers game was limited to juniors and seniors only. And considering it was summer, and the seniors graduated last month, I narrowed it down to guys who were juniors this last year.

Chase and Jeremy were there on the right, of course. But also... someone I couldn't place right away. I had to rely on the caption below the picture.

Drew Gottlieb. Someone I knew by name only, maybe having one conversation with previously. I chided myself for not remembering the name right away, as it was a skill I honed over the years. But to my defense, I couldn't remember him ever wearing glasses like he was in this picture.

Slamming the book shut, I put the three names into my spreadsheet and moved on.

My next thought was from the most recent trivia session. My research paper on Gandhi. Did my secret admirer add that question because they knew about my paper? If so, then he had to have been in my Geography class freshman year.

I had to think hard to determine what guys were in that class. It seemed like forever ago, but a few names came back to me.

Josh and Marcus again. But also Davis Maguire, Connor Grey, Joey Richards, and Andrew Del Marco.

They all went onto the list, excluding putting Josh and Marcus twice. Considering they weren't directly related to a clue, their likelihood wouldn't increase because of this.

Now it was onto the clues themselves. The first one, about close but far and shadows, left me absolutely stumped. There was nothing specific to go on. The vagueness of it frustrated me and provided no logical information.

So I skipped it and went to the second clue. Flip-flops and beaches. This one at least gave me something solid.

Flip-flops. Who wore those? Swimmers. Well, a lot of people in the summer, but outside of that, swimmers.

Grabbing the yearbook again, I flipped to the athletics section and scanned until I found the boy's swim team. Using my finger as a guide, I read all the names until the ones of juniors jumped out at me.

Jesse, Theo, Matt, Mike, Brett, Bernie, and Tyler.

My mind was already overwhelmed with names, but I added them all to the list. The last part of the clue was about the beach. Considering almost everyone wore flip-flops to the beach, or went barefoot, I crossed that option off as a possible spot for suspects. The only people I would think of were the beach lifeguards, and they were usually barefoot.

I had twenty names on my list and it was only the start. Two clues down, and who knew how many more to go.

Glaring at the screen, I tried to pull a few names out that would seem the most likely. Two jumped out at me—Chase and Josh.

Chase was in my study group, along with Mya, Emilia, and Tucker. Josh was more of a school friend; we didn't hang outside of school really.

But... could that relate to the shadows comment? Did he feel like he was in the shadows because we didn't cross paths naturally? And he was ready to play—it was summer. Everyone was ready to play, and I bet he had been at the beach yesterday. There was a group of guys further down the sand playing volleyball. I just never looked hard enough to determine who was there.

A flutter of excitement built in my stomach. It had to be him. So far, it all made sense. Logistically, it was correct.

My brain went into overdrive as I continued to jot down all the ways that it had to be Josh Nichols.

He was in multiple of my classes over the years. I knew for a fact that he voted for me to be student body president—he specifically stopped me in the hallway to tell me so on voting day. And there was the one time last year that he gave me free ice cream when Skye and I went to the Dairy Bar, where he used to work.

A slow smile spread across my face as the feeling of satisfaction washed through me. Could I be the first girl to solve the secret admirer mystery this early? Potentially.

I didn't want to showboat though, and I needed to collect some more data to be sure. But so far, everything lined up.

*D*ad rounded the corner just as I let out a small groan, rubbing the soles of my feet, careful to avoid the blister that was building on top of another blister. The heels I bought were a sham; I should have worn slippers.

"I'll be ready to go in about thirty minutes," he said. "Do you need something to do or are you wrapping up?"

I glanced around. "I guess I could use something to do."

Dad headed down the hall toward his office. "Great! The kitchen can use some tidying, and the conference room needs a bit of straightening up."

He didn't look back to see the glare coming from me, but the distant sound of his laughter said he knew his comments didn't please me.

I didn't hesitate, though. If cleaning the kitchen meant my foot was in the door for the future, then I would clean it every day. Everyone had to start somewhere.

"Ready to go, kiddo?" Dad said, as I put a new garbage bag in the bin, tucking it under the sink.

I brushed off my hands and surveyed my work. "Yup. All finished."

Dad glanced around. "Looks great. By the way, we have a cleaning crew that comes every night." He burst out laughing as he slung an arm around my shoulders.

I narrowed my eyes and sucked in a deep breath. But then, I switched my mindset, just to throw him off. "That's alright. Cleaning gave me something to do and some time to think. Plus, it makes it a more inviting space for all the employees and shows strength of character."

Dad sighed. "You are going to make a great lawyer someday, Spence. Always keeping everyone on their toes and showing them what they miss."

I tossed my bag into the backseat next to Dad's briefcase, jumping when my phone buzzed in my palm.

Dad laughed again, pointing at my phone. "You learned to keep that thing on silent now, huh?"

I bit my cheek to keep from blushing. "During work hours, absolutely. Honestly, I keep it on silent most of the time anyway. That day was... unfortunate."

We got in and Dad started the car, pulling out of the parking garage and onto the main road. Home wasn't too far, but far enough that I had time to deal with whatever I missed while working.

Three texts and a few social media posts greeted me on my home screen. But that wasn't what I looked at right away.

Trivia for a Clue sent you a message: New Entry

My heart skipped a beat. It had been a few days since the beach. I even had time to complete the rest of my spreadsheet, rankings and all.

Josh was still at the top of the list, light years above everyone else. Even though the swimmers held high priority because of the flip-flop clue, Josh still reigned over them at a whopping 5 out of 5 on the likability scale.

I glanced at Dad, as if he could sense my nervous energy. But he continued driving, nodding his head to the song on the radio, completely oblivious to me.

After debating whether I had enough time to go through all five rounds, I ended up putting my phone down. It would have to wait. Besides, I bet the new clue would just lead to Josh anyway.

Once dinner ended, I excused myself to my room, fully prepared to tackle the questions. Before I could get started, however, my phone buzzed once again.

> **TUCKER:** I have a craving.

> **ME:** Are you pregnant?

> **TUCKER:** That's really original. No, I want a three-scoop sundae, extra hot fudge, no whip, with nuts and two cherries.

> **ME:** That's... specific.

> **TUCKER:** I told you I had a craving. My cravings are never vague.

ME: Well, what are you going to do about that?

TUCKER: Me? Nothing. You? Are going to come get me and take me to the Dairy Bar.

ME: Umm... nothing in that sentence started with the letter p.

TUCKER: I know plenty of p words. Want one?

ME: You have a dirty mind, Tuck. Be ready in ten.

I snorted as I read Tucker's message. Though we didn't work out as a couple, he was still a really good friend, and his sense of humor never failed to bring a smile to my face.

Now that he mentioned his craving, I had one of my own. Grabbing my phone and a light-weight zip-up, I bolted toward the back door.

"I'm going out for ice cream! Want me to bring anything back for you guys?" I shouted toward Mom and Dad, who were watching TV in the den.

They shouted back, but I couldn't really understand them. A moment later, my phone buzzed.

MOM: One scoop of cookie dough for me, and two scoops of chocolate for your father, please. Thank you, sweetheart.

I replied with a thumbs up and a kiss emoji before jumping in my car and heading out. Tucker only lived a few minutes away, which is probably why he chose me to target his craving toward.

He came flying out of his front door a second after I honked in his driveway. We kept some small talk until we got to the ice cream shop. He had no idea how giddy I was to see Josh in person. It would be a great opportunity to keep an eye on body language or nervousness.

"Josh! I didn't know you would be working tonight!" I said, hopefully in a tone that didn't give away my downright lie. Honestly, I did think he had quit the Dairy Bar a while ago, but with some internet stalking over the past few days, I saw he was still around.

"I picked up extra shifts. I need the money. Besides, the owner's son decided to go on some sort of 'finding myself' trip, so they needed the help," he answered with a grin. His uniform baseball hat sat backwards on his head, allowing a tuft of hair to peek out over his forehead. "What can I get you guys?"

Tucker got his order set, then I grabbed a small vanilla in a cup with a little hot fudge on top. All the while, I tried to be sly, watching Josh out of the corner of my eye.

"You're missing out, Spence. This is where it's at," Tucker said, pointing his spoon at his sundae. Just looking at it made my insides jittery. If I ate all of that this late into the evening, I would be on a sugar high until breakfast.

I laughed. "You enjoy."

Just then, a thought popped into my mind. I had a game to play, and if I did it in front of Josh... maybe he would give himself away. "Hey, Tuck... want to help me with something?"

The game said that if I was with someone, I could use them to help answer the questions. I might as well use that to my advantage.

Tucker lifted his brows and scooped another bite into his mouth. "Yeah, sure. What's up?"

I moved my cup away, placing my phone on the table and opening up the trivia app.

"What's that?" His genuine surprise over the app didn't surprise me. I didn't really think Tucker was behind the game, even though I kept him on the list as a possibility anyway.

"I'm surprised Emilia didn't spill the beans, but the secret admirer game *didn't* break for the summer..." I winked and sent him a grin.

"Yes!" Josh shouted from behind the counter, fist pumping the air. "My streak stays alive!"

Tucker and I both whipped our heads in his direction, wondering what he was going on about. He hurried from behind the counter, grabbed a chair, turned it backwards, and sat at the table with us.

"Your streak?" Tucker asked.

"Somehow, all secret admirer contestants end up in the shop to work out clues." He shrugged, like it made the most sense. It seemed rather suspicious to me, but I pushed on. Giving out the questions would be more of a tell.

"Anyway," I started, pointing at the phone again, "my secret admirer made an app and—"

"He *made* an app? Well, that takes out a good portion

of Ryder students," Josh snorted. So far, he was doing a decent job at acting like he didn't know what this was. Maybe he was going a bit overkill in order to divert attention away from himself?

"It's a trivia app. I have to answer five random trivia questions in order to get the clue."

"How many have you done so far?" Tucker asked, leaning with his elbows on the table.

"Two."

"Do you have a suspect list?" Josh raised his eyebrows as if he thought I would tell him everyone on my list. Was he asking because he knew he was on it, or because he had no idea what was happening?

"It's long. The clues have been vague," I grimaced. I *hated* vagueness. Tucker laughed, knowing exactly how it bothered me.

"Let's play then! Maybe we can help and narrow down that list," Tucker said. "What do we do?"

I opened the app and went through the parts in the beginning before getting to the first question.

What famous magician died on Halloween day 1926?

"Houdini," Josh said confidently. Tucker and I stared at him. It was an odd piece of knowledge to know. Unless he made the clues...

He shrugged. "My uncle's a magician. He taught me a few things over the years, and knowing magician's secrets means you have to understand the history behind the tricks. No bigger piece of magician history than Houdini."

There was no need to argue; it was the most reasonable choice for me, too. I clicked on Houdini, and it jumped onto the board next to the number one.

"Oh man, Uncle Josh is going to flip when I tell him I actually used something he taught me for once."

Tucker furrowed his brows. "Your uncle has the same name as you?"

Josh chuckled. "Yeah. Long story."

"And we don't have time for it, unfortunately," I interrupted, already moving on to question two.

> *In the movie Home Alone, what animal did Buzz keep as a pet?*

"Did your secret admirer know that you would be with us when he made this? Because the answer is tarantula. One hundred percent. I watch that movie every single Christmas," Tucker answered.

It was a little suspicious. Did Josh say something to someone who then suggested Tucker to get ice cream with me? was this all part of a larger plot I was unaware of? I shrugged as I clicked on the answer. "No idea. Just good luck, I suppose? Next question."

> *Who wrote 1818's "Frankenstein"?*

"I thought these were supposed to get harder, not easier," I mumbled under my breath as I hit Mary Shelley's name quickly. The answer appeared on the board and we moved on.

Dear Spencer

What is the state animal of Florida?

I paused. Tucker drummed his fingers on the table. Josh let out a puff of air and pushed back from his chair.

"Um... they all sound correct," he said.

"Alligator. Panther. Dolphin." I listed the options out loud, even though we were all staring at them. "Let's take dolphin out. It seems a little implausible for an oceanic animal to be a state animal." Tucker shrugged, but I made up my mind.

"Okay... my bet is on alligator. I mean, when you think of Florida, it's like the first animal that comes to mind, right?"

Josh nodded. "Makes sense. But Florida also has the Panthers as their hockey team."

I stared him down, debating in my head. I racked my brain trying to see if any other teams used their state animal as a sports mascot, but came up short. "I'm still thinking alligator."

Incorrect. The correct answer is: Panther.

"Tough choice. Do you have to get them all right?" Josh asked. Again, was he asking because he knew or didn't know? This back-and-forth game was making my brain hurt. He was my top suspect, but I could barely function right now. My mind was so focused on trying to catch any little thing that there was no space for anything else.

I shook my head. "No, only three of five, which we already did. But we have to finish the game."

What clouds are thick and puffy and can some-times turn into thunderstorms?

The options popped up, each word looking suspiciously like the others.

"Cumulo... cumbla... crumble cake, final answer," Tucker said, struggling to pronounce words.

My heart sunk. I didn't know this answer either. Even though we already got three of five correct, I didn't want to go down as failing two options. It was bad enough when Skye missed the one the other day, but to miss two? Unheard of. That's a sixty percent average. A D⁻, in grading terms. I was not a D⁻ student.

All I could do was take an educated guess, though. How educated was the problem, because all the answers looked the same.

"I... I don't know," I muttered. Tucker glanced at my panic-stricken face, grabbed the phone, and punched in a random answer.

Incorrect. The correct answer is: Cumulus.

My breath hitched, but before I could react, the screen changed. There was no confetti, but it did flip to the notebook paper with the text.

Great job. But beware—the questions will be get-ting harder. Multiple choice answers are gone. Good luck...

Your clue for today is: This may be an early admis-sion, but I could write an essay on our tumultuous relationship. What you don't know is how you fill in all the bubbles on my list.

"Umm, what kind of clue is that?" Tucker asked, handing the phone back to me. I clicked out of the app and slipped it into my purse.

I sighed. "I have no idea. Honestly, most of my suspects have been coming from other areas, like who could build an app, or who knows I love trivia."

Josh gave me a half-grin. I sensed a little bit of pity in his tone, but brushed it off. "Wish I could be more help, but my girlfriend just arrived..." He pointed to the parking lot, where a girl I didn't recognize was headed toward the door, a massive smile on her face.

"You have a girlfriend?" I exclaimed as the bell over the door jingled.

"As of a week ago, sure do!" he answered, slipping his arm around her waist. She looped both of her arms around his torso and squeezed. My heart plummeted.

"Hi, I'm Jessica. I go to Parkdale High," she said in a soft, sweet voice. Parkdale was a few towns over, about thirty minutes away.

I picked my jaw up off the floor just in time to give her a smile and turn my attention back to Josh. My now *ex*-main suspect.

"I should go. Josh, can you grab those orders for my parents before the crazy starts?" I squeaked out, hopefully in a tone that didn't scream, *how could I be so wrong?*

Josh whipped up the ice cream in a flash, sending Tucker and I on our way while he chilled at a table with Jessica.

"So, who are you adding to the list?" Tucker said as we reached the car.

I shrugged. "No idea. I'll have to analyze the clue a bit more. Did you know Josh had a girlfriend?"

Tucker bit his lower lip. "Nope. But I also don't know that much about him period."

Disappointment settled in me. Not only was I completely wrong about Josh, but now it was time to go back to the spreadsheet and figure out what I missed by being so fixated on him being my Secret Admirer.

"Something about the wording is throwing me. Fill my bubbles? Who says stuff like that? Tumultuous? That sounds like an SAT word." Tucker was still rambling on as I drove, even though I hadn't really been listening for a moment.

My breath hitched and my eyes widened, but I didn't say a word. Tucker's thought sparked an idea, but I wanted to get home and in front of my spreadsheet first.

"Thanks for indulging me on a spur-of-the-moment idea, Spence," Tucker said as he climbed out of the car once we reached his house. I waved and backed down the driveway.

Mom and Dad were asleep when I got home. After dropping their orders in the freezer, I took the stairs two at a time to my room.

Flipping my laptop open, I stared at the list in front of me.

More than one person's ranking would change after tonight, that was for sure.

9 didn't have to add any new names to my list, just update some of the current ones, especially the likability factors.

Josh was taken out—highlighted in red to indicate that he was once involved, but no longer an option.

The swimmers had a head start—they were all two's already because of their relation to clue number two. Everyone else was at a one, since they didn't relate directly to a clue at all.

But now, multiple people bumped up likability. What Tucker said inspired me, and gave me a little leeway into creating more reasonability into the clue.

Tumultuous was, in fact, an SAT word. One I remembered from taking the SAT prep class earlier this year. And multiple people on my list were in that class with me.

Members in my SAT prep class that were pre-existing as suspects already included Josh, Marcus, Theo, and Connor.

Connor was now at a two, for being in my geography class and SAT prep. But he was an easy one to take off the list since he also had a girlfriend at the moment. I didn't delete him, because deletion was a final act, and we could never rule out anyone until the very end, but he got put in red as well.

Theo and Marcus were the ones that increased the most and caused me the most confusion. If I were to go based on personal opinion alone, they would both be at zeroes. I barely knew Theo, and Marcus... well, was Marcus.

The other part of the clue that stood out to me was the early decision part. Many people had already made their decision on which college to attend, even though we just finished our junior year.

Marcus, Jeremy, and Chase had already received their acceptance letters and were committed. After putting that into the list, it put Jeremy and Chase at three's—they were both part of the computer club too and had the highest probability of making an app.

But Marcus and Theo... Theo had two clues officially tied to him, with being a swimmer and in my SAT prep class. That made his probability a four, even though he didn't have any other reasonings. Clues weighed more than opinion.

Marcus threw me. He was on the trivia committee, in my geography class, SAT prep, and early decision. He also was at a four out of five, even though he only related to one specific clue.

But we butted heads more than we agreed on anything. Every year we were at each other's throats, back and forth with running against each other, and always pinned against each other in debate. He loved to sass me more than anyone I knew. There was just no way he was behind this unless it was a prank. And I knew him well enough to say he wouldn't go into all this trouble for a prank. Max Newman, maybe. Marcus Edmond? Never.

His name also went in the red with Connor and Josh. It made almost as little sense as Theo, who I had never had a full conversation with in the three years of high school we've completed. But at least I knew Theo didn't despise me and everything I stood for, which was clear from Marcus' attempts at smear campaigns over the years.

So *why* were my top candidates the least likely to be the actual secret admirer? A few of the three's I could see being genuine suspects. Chase, Jeremy, and Theo now topped the list.

Theo... was there just something there I hadn't seen before? Was he in the shadows, now wanting to play? It made sense, using the secret admirer game to get at someone the guy held a long-standing crush on but never actually approached the girl prior.

Theo... sure he was a jock, but maybe opposites could attract? I had no idea what his ambitions were in life besides swimming, but I was up for a challenge.

And just like that, Theo Kaminsky shot to the top and was my next main suspect.

I sighed, tearing my gaze away from the computer, looking at my bed longingly. The sugar from the ice cream kept me awake longer than I wanted to be, especially after a day of work. I shut the laptop and trudged my way to the bathroom to get ready for bed. In the back of my mind, I knew I would be up for another few hours, mentally debating the smallest detail over every suspect.

The next clue didn't come for another three days. So far, between the days and times, there was no pattern to find. I could never expect when a new game was coming in; it always surprised me. Every time I heard my phone beep or felt it vibrate in my pocket, my heart leaped into my throat, thinking it would be another clue.

This time, it was in the quiet of my own bedroom after I spent the day at the office with Dad again. Sandra even complimented me on my timely delivery of files and the organization of the break room. Another partner let me sit in on a non-confidential meeting, and asked to see my notes afterwards.

Both Dad and I came home with our chins high, feeling proud of ourselves for different reasons. He must have texted Mom throughout the day too, because she made our favorite dinner tonight, and even brownies for dessert.

It wasn't that late at night, almost nine o'clock, but I was wiped. Instead of a half day, I went with Dad for a full day, getting up around seven and not coming home until five thirty. I could barely keep my eyes open as I scrolled flipped through a book. I re-read the same page three times before I decided to call it quits and get some sleep.

But the moment I returned from brushing my teeth, my phone chimed.

Trivia for a Clue sent you a message: New Entry

I took a flying leap onto my bed, rolling over so I laid on my back, my phone hovering over my face.

After adjusting my glasses from the tussle, I clicked into the app, skipping through all the stuff at the start until I got to the questions. I briefly saw the note stating multiple choices were gone, which made me nervous, but excitement took over.

What major city hosts the island prison of Alcatraz?

I huffed a laugh. Too easy. He said these questions would be difficult, but so far, we've done a great job. There were a few incorrect, but nothing too outrageous. I typed on San Francisco, and it flew to the bar next to number one. Easy peasy.

Who was the first European to land in America?

My heart skipped a beat. Off the bat, I was supposed to say Christopher Columbus, which had been ingrained in us since elementary school, but I knew that was wrong. However,... no other names were jumping out at me. There were no lifelines to use, no guessing allowed. I had one chance, and one chance only.

And I chose wrong. I wrote in the only other name I could think of besides Columbus, even though I knew it was after his time, Hernan Cortes.

Incorrect. The correct answer is: Leif Erikson, in the 10th century.

Before I could contemplate the letdown, the next question popped up.

Who did Abraham Lincoln face in a series of debates in 1858?

Again, easy. Either the person behind the app knew I had been on the debate team since freshman year, or they were oblivious. I entered Stephen Douglas quickly and confidently.

Atychiphobia, Kakorrahaphobia or Kakorraphiophobia is the irrational fear of what?

Phobias. One of my major gripes about trivia. The names of phobias all looked alike, all had too many letters, and I couldn't pronounce any of them. The only one I knew was arachnophobia, the fear of spiders. For all I knew, these could be the fear of clowns or the fear of grass.

Which is what I entered. I had two questions right, and one wrong. If I got this one wrong, I still had a chance at winning with the last question.

Incorrect. The correct answer is: Failure.

That felt like a smack in the face. One of *my* fears in life was failure, and here it was, in a question I *failed*. It didn't get any more ironic, or pitiful, than that. At least now I had a name to put to my phobia.

Taking a deep breath, I tried to center myself and

focus. I had to get the last question right in order to get the clue. If I didn't, I had to wait for another chance.

In 1963, the New York Zoo's Great Ape House was home to the "most dangerous animal in the world" exhibit. What was the exhibit?

I mentally went through all the apes I knew offhand—gorillas, chimps, orangutans, gibbons. Which one of those would be considered the most dangerous back in 1963?

It had to be gorillas. The male silverback could easily dismember a person, or other animals. They also are the largest living primate. I typed in gorillas and held my breath.

Incorrect. The correct answer is: A mirror.

A *mirror*? A mirror? How... what... It took a moment for my brain to catch up to the idea of a mirror in an exhibit. Humans. Humans were the most dangerous animal in the world and in the same classification as apes.

I lost. The note paper on the screen appeared, with the text showing up as if it was being typed out.

Better luck next time. Your next chance at an attempt for a clue will be in 12-24 hours. The questions will be different. Don't lose faith—just keep swimming!

The app went back to the home screen, but I didn't stick around. I tossed the phone to the other side of the bed and curled up on my side.

Failure wasn't something I took lightly. The normal process was to grieve, beat myself up mentally for a short time, recoup, go over every minute detail, then learn from the mistakes and move on. Sometimes it only took a day, sometimes longer.

This one... I didn't necessarily want to grieve, but I was upset with myself. He said it would be harder, and without multiple choice, it was near impossible. There was no way to even have an educated guess without options.

I fell asleep, still thinking about each question and how I could have tried to analyze them differently to come up with the correct answer.

I groaned, rolling over and smacking my phone as if it were an alarm clock. My mind had been wired last night, giving me a rather uneasy night of sleep. The last thing I wanted was an early wake up call. But the buzzing didn't stop. Mostly because it wasn't an alarm clock, it was a string of texts.

> **EMILIA:** Rise and shine, girlfriend! I hope you're up. We're meeting at the festival in thirty. Can you bring extra sunscreen? I forgot and am already in the car.

> **EMILIA:** You didn't forget about Family Festival Day, did you?

> **EMILIA:** Spencer! Wake up! If you were up, you would have answered me by now.

She had a point. I was a rather fast responder, mainly because I liked the issues dealt with immediately instead of having to think about it all day. If I could answer an email or respond to a message right then, I did.

> **ME:** I'm up, I'm up. Well, I am now. I'll be ready!

After counting to five, I jumped out of bed and trudged to the bathroom. Since we would be outside in the heat and humidity today, I didn't bother showering now. The probability of sweating and looking like a mess by the end of the day was high. A shower when I returned home would be a must.

After gathering my already frizzing hair into a high pony, I made sure to put some wax on the nose piece of my glasses, in an attempt to convince them to stay put no matter how gross it got outside. Then, I dumped other random items into a large tote—sunscreen, a book, snacks, a hat, and whatever else I convinced myself we needed.

As soon as I pulled up, the stress I didn't realize I had been holding in my shoulders wore away. Seeing Emilia in her massive straw sunhat and a big grin calmed me.

"You look stressed," was the first thing she said as I opened my car door.

"Spencer is always stressed. It would be more shocking to say she *didn't* look stressed," Chase said from behind her. He popped his head over her shoulder and smiled at me, lowering his sunglasses and giving me a wink.

I rolled my eyes at him. "Why are you here again? Don't you have to be home to listen to your police scanner or something?"

Chase stepped aside, opening his arms for a hug. I wasn't a hugger, and he knew it, and he used it against me every single time I saw him. "I heard you were coming, so of course I had to be here."

I tightened when his arms wrapped around me. Chase McNeill had hugged me dozens of times, but right now, with that comment, it made me freeze. He was on my suspect list. And though he wasn't at the top, he was close enough for me to need to keep an eye on, which made his comment suspicious.

"Why are you stressed? You should be ready to have fun!" Emilia said. "It's summer!"

"I was up late. Long day at the office with Dad, and then another trivia—" I clamped my lips shut, not sure if I should mention the fact that I had a chance at a clue last night, but lost. She would want details, and then I would have to go into the suspect list and everything, which would turn into stress again.

Instead of prying, she leaned over into the back seat and handed me my tote bag. After locking the car, we made our way toward the entrance booth. Waiting right in front of it was none other than Mr. Ice Cream Craving himself, Tucker.

"Spence! Glad you could join us. It's been a few days, have you gotten any more—"

I gave one curt shake of my head while glaring at him, forcing him to cut himself off mid-sentence. But it was too late—Emilia and Chase heard, and were now waiting for more.

"I bought all of our tickets!" Tucker exclaimed, waving them in the air as a distraction.

"Gotten any more what? Any more clues?" Emilia asked, turning toward me. Her smile stretched across her cheeks, lifting the bottom of her sunglasses higher on her face.

I ignored her for a moment, digging into my bag for the baseball hat I brought. I shoved it onto my head, pulling my ponytail through the back.

"Clues for what?" Chase asked, snatching his ticket out of Tucker's hand.

The three of us stared at him for a moment. "You don't know that Spencer was chosen for Secret Admirer's this month?" Emilia looked at Chase with her brows furrowed in concern.

We walked through the gates and headed toward food first. Even though it was early, we would be snacking all day long, mostly on the junkiest food we could get.

"Um, no. No one told me! How was I supposed to know if no one told me!" Chase cried.

I handed over a few bills to the vender and passed out a cone of cotton candy to everyone. It's how our group worked, missing Mya of course. But she was leaving to spend a few weeks at her grandparent's house before heading to theater camp next month, so she couldn't come today.

The five of us had been a study group since freshman year, but were more than that. We were best friends, and worked so well as a team, it was almost scary how in tune with each other we were.

Chase stuffed a wad of pink cotton candy in his mouth, barely chewing before speaking again. "Okay, so you're the it girl this month. Nothing new for you to be on top.

But I bet you have a list of suspects already, so who's the guy? Have you figured it out yet?"

I bit my lip, considering how much I should give away. I definitely did *not* want to tell anyone that I failed the round of trivia last night. They may be my closest friends, but admitting it to them would be painful. Losing the round hurt enough, I didn't need to add to it.

However... I could always use their opinions. "Well, honestly, I already eliminated a few people, but there is someone I have suspicions about."

"You have a list?" Emilia gasped. "And you didn't tell me? Who's on it?"

"Oddly enough, a few names are topping the list. Theo Kaminsky is among them."

She paused. "Theo... like the captain of the guy's swim team? That's..."

"Weird, right?" I finished for her. Her face screwed up, her nose doing the thing where it bunches in the middle and makes her freckles smoosh together.

"Yeah. I mean..."

"Wait, Theo Kaminsky? The guy who can't even do basic addition?" Tucker asked before tossing his now empty cone into the trash bin to his right.

I sighed. "Yes, but—"

"Spencer, how the heck did you come up with *Theo Kaminsky* on the top of your leaderboard?" Chase interrupted. "And why would you even consider such a prospect?"

Telling him that he and Tucker were also both on my list seemed to be a petty move at this point. Sure, Theo wasn't the smartest person in our school, but that didn't mean he didn't have other qualities about him that were endearing.

I had no idea what those qualities were... yet. There was still plenty of time to get to know him personally, though.

Holding up a hand, I stopped all of them in their tracks. "He fit the clues. He's on the swim team and in my SAT prep class. I think he might have been at trivia night during freshman year community fundraiser?" The last part came out like a question because I had just pulled it out of thin air; there was absolutely no validity behind it.

Emilia opened her mouth to argue, but I kept going. "Besides, stranger pairings have happened before. Remember Rachel and Tom from last year?" I shot them all a pointed look, reminding them that there have been weirder things than me and Theo within this game.

Tucker pursed his lips. "No offense, Spence, but I just can't see it being Theo..." he trailed off, but raised his hand to point to a booth in front of us.

We all turned, watching as all six foot something of pure muscle that was Theo Kaminsky chugged an entire bottle of Sprite not fifteen feet in front of us.

And then let out the largest burp I had ever heard.

Emilia and I both cringed while Chase and Tucker fought hard to hold back their laughter. It didn't work well, though, because we were spotted.

"Lookie here, it's the president! Do we have to salute? Curtsey? What's the protocol, prezzie?" Theo's best friend and teammate, Jesse, exclaimed.

Inside, I was dying. But outside, I kept my composure and plastered a smile on my face. "None of the above, thanks. Just passing through here."

My group walked toward them, looking as if we were going to be able to walk right by without incident. But, that wasn't quite the case.

"President? Who's a president?" Theo asked before burping once again. "And man, I am *never* doing that challenge again." He patted his stomach, letting out another belch. Then, he lifted up his shirt—a T-shirt with the arms cut off, and the holes big enough that we could see down to his navel from the side—and rubbed his washboard six-pack abs.

Jesse backhanded him in the chest, forcing him to drop the shirt and smack Jesse back. "Dude!"

"President Spencer Matthews, you idiot. Didn't you vote for her? She's *right in front of you*, moron."

I tilted my head, giving Jesse a grateful smile.

"Uh, vote? I didn't vote for anyone. No, wait, I voted Marcus! He said we could party all the time and that he'd get fast food in the cafeteria."

"He never said such things," I countered, squaring my shoulders as if ready for a debate.

Theo scratched his head, his shaggy, dirty blonde locks already coated with sweat. At least, I hoped it was sweat. "Huh. Well, that's what I remembered, so I voted for him. Who are you again?"

I opened my mouth to speak, but Chase and Emilia both pulled me away by the arms. Tucker said something to the boys about our departure, but I didn't catch it.

"Sorry to say I told you so, but... yeah, we totally told you so," Chase said once we were far enough away.

I glared at him. "He didn't even know who I was!" I spat out with more of a harsh tone than I meant to.

Chase shrugged. "Doesn't surprise me."

"Or me," Emilia chimed in.

"Or me," Tucker finished up.

Huffing out a breath, I folded my arms over my chest. "Let's go. Maybe we can hit the beach and get a good spot before the concert tonight."

Every family festival finished with a concert on the beach. But not the normal one we usually hung out at— the one a town over, where they could set up bleachers and everything since there was more room. It filled up quick, so getting a good spot early was key.

Besides, I had no reason to stay here anymore. Not while knowing Theo lurked around the corners, his abs and the soundtrack of his burps haunting me.

It was past dinner once the music finally stopped. Since it was a family festival, it all ended right around seven in the evening, allowing those with younger children the chance to enjoy it as well.

Most of the high schoolers stuck around for the bonfire, but I needed some quality time with my laptop. After the disaster that was Theo today, and Josh the other day, I had some serious data to input and things to consider. Every time I've had a top contender so far, it's been a massive bust. Was I missing something right in front of me? What wasn't I seeing?

I said goodbye to Chase, Tucker, and Emilia, promising to meet up with them again later in the week and to let them know if any more clues came through. Hopefully I would have good news to text them in a group chat later tonight, if the chance for redemption ever came through.

Only five minutes into my drive home, my phone chimed with a message. I fumbled with my bag on the seat next to me, unable to find it right away. Normally I would leave it in my bag and not look until I got to a full stop, but I knew what it was.

Once I got a hold of it, I held it in front of my face for confirmation.

Trivia for a Clue sent you a message: New Entry

It was the last thing I saw.

The bright lights over my eyes hurt my head. I tried to raise my hand to block them, but I couldn't. *Why couldn't I move my arm?*

"Stay still, sweetie. We're putting an IV in right now," an unfamiliar voice said to my left.

An attempt to move my head to see who spoke was also unsuccessful. There was something strapped to my head, blocking me from moving it.

"Whaaa..." I managed to get out. My mouth was so dry, I could barely speak.

"Spencer, is it? Spencer Matthews of Robinwood Lane?" A middle-aged woman with short blonde hair and worry lines across her forehead leaned over me, directly in view.

I couldn't nod, so I blinked instead.

"My name is Amanda. I'm an EMT. You were in a little accident. You were awake when we got to you, but you passed out once in the ambulance. It's normal. When the shock starts to wear off, your body can sometimes shut down in order for it to... well, think of it like a computer. Too much going on, it overheats, and shuts down for a reboot. You've been rebooted." She smiled at me like I would find it a funny joke.

"Acci... dent?" I mouthed, mustering up as much strength to get the words out as possible.

Amanda nodded. "Yes, I'm afraid so. According to the police, you crossed the middle line, into oncoming traffic. Then you swerved to avoid the car headed toward you, over corrected, and ended up in the ditch. We think that's where you hit your head and your foot slammed into the footwell. It's swelling up something gnarly, so I'm thinking there may be a small fracture. We'll be at Bella General in about two minutes."

An accident. I got into an accident. *How* had I gotten into an accident? I had a stellar driving record. I barely even sped.

"I found this nearby..." Amanda said, dangling my phone over my face. "Swiped it for ya. I know teenagers these days and their phone addictions. But I must say... was this the reason for your crash?"

I stared up at it, trying to figure out the last thing I remembered. The boat. Emilia. Ryan. Laying out. Lunch. The dock.

A burst of pain flooded my head, and I cringed, unable to focus again.

"That'll be a potential concussion. They'll evaluate you at the hospital once they clear your spine. I'm going to tuck this in your purse, which I also grabbed for you." She gave me a wink as the ambulance slowed down.

"You are one lucky girl, Spencer Matthews. Put the phone away next time. I don't want to see you in this ambulance again, you hear me?"

If I could have nodded, I would have. Instead, I blinked, hoping my appreciation came through.

Mom and Dad weren't too far behind the ambulance. The EMTs put me into a room in the emergency department, and my parents showed up not ten minutes later.

After they arrived, I had a scan to clear my spine, and then they took off the collar, allowing me to move freely once more. The throbbing pain in my foot worried the doctors, and they took me for X-rays on that as well.

Six hours, one diagnosed concussion, and a fractured foot later, Mom and Dad could take me home. I had strict instructions not to look at any type of screen, and to follow up with an orthopedist for my foot tomorrow.

Mom shuffled through the papers in the car, exhaustion settling in for all of us. "There's a lot to go over here, Spencer. Concussions are serious business."

I nodded, but didn't answer. Everything was sore. My mind was hurt. All I wanted to do was sleep.

Once we got home, Mom helped me to my room using the crutch the hospital provided. She then helped me out of the pair of scrubs a nice nurse swiped for me, since I had crashed while in my bikini and cover up. After a quick brush of my teeth, I teetered into bed.

"Goodnight, sweetheart. I'm so glad you're alright," Mom whispered. She gave me a kiss on the head and smoothed my hair back.

That was the last thing I heard before falling into a deep, deep sleep.

Both of my parents were downstairs when I woke up, which was odd, as it was almost two in the afternoon. We didn't get home until just after three this morning. I wasn't sure why I assumed Dad would be going into work after that.

"Um, hi?" I whispered as I made my way into the kitchen. My stomach growled, reminding me that I hadn't eaten anything since lunch on Ryan's boat yesterday. Over twenty-four hours ago, to be exact.

Mom jumped to her feet and rushed over to help me into a chair. "How are you feeling, sweetie? How did you get down here?" She glanced between me and my crutch, which I managed to use to hobble down the stairs. It took more energy than I had, but I didn't want to burden my parents.

"Spence... we can help you. Let us help," Dad said from the other side of the table. His tablet was open to the latest news, and a cup of coffee sat beside it. On any normal day, it would look like a normal breakfast scene. Except it was after lunch today. Both of them must have slept in late too.

"Oh, you know I didn't sleep. I was up almost every hour checking on you," Mom said, giving me a knowing glance. Our brains were eerily similar, and she seemed to know things I was thinking without me needed to vocalize it.

"Coffee? Tea? Hot cocoa? Milk? Cereal? What can I get you, sweetheart?" Mom asked, opening cupboards to show me the options I knew were already there.

"Umm..." I started just as my stomach let out another large rumble.

"Eggs and bacon, it is. Dear, can you get a few pans out for me?" Mom directed toward Dad as she dove into the fridge for ingredients. "And don't bother arguing, baby girl, it's a done deal."

I clamped my mouth shut and stared out the window. My head had a dull ache, and my foot was still throbbing. We were supposed to go to the doctor today to see if it needed a full cast or a boot. I crossed my fingers for a boot, so I could at least walk on it and not have to rely on the crutches or outside help.

The scrambled eggs and extra-crispy bacon Mom made were heaven in my mouth. I had multiple servings, which she must have expected, since she made almost a dozen eggs for the three of us, and a whole pound of bacon.

"I can clean—" I attempted to say, but Dad cut me off.

"Nope. You sit and drink your coffee. I'll clean up." He stood tall, planting his hands on his hips and looking off into the distance as if offering to clean up made him some sort of superhero.

Mom and I both laughed. "I won't complain about that!" she said. I took a sip of the iced coffee Mom made, allowing the cool liquid to travel through my body as I slumped back in the chair.

"What time is the appointment?" I asked. Before she could answer, the doorbell rang.

"I'll get it!" Mom shouted, as if anyone else was available to answer it.

I couldn't see around the corner to tell who was at the door, but as soon as she opened it and started talking, it was clear.

"Is she okay?" Emilia's voice traveled through the house.

"Yeah, we haven't heard anything except a car crash!" Tucker followed behind.

"Kitchen!" I shouted, telling them I indeed was alive, and to come find me.

"Oh my gosh, Spencer!" Em gushed as she flew into the kitchen. She put down a large bouquet of flowers on the table in front of me and flung her arms around my neck. "Are you alright? What happened?"

Tucker settled himself into Dad's chair, resting his elbows on his knees as he leaned forward. "Glad to see you still kickin'," he said with a grin.

I smiled back, trying to make them feel comfortable despite their worry. "Stupid mistake. Crashed the car, hit my head, and bashed my foot against the foot well."

Downplaying the seriousness of the situation was a power move I took out when I needed everyone to remain calm. I didn't overlook the severity, but didn't want them to worry.

"Do you have a concussion?" Tucker asked. I nodded slowly.

"Oh my gosh, this is all my fault!" Emilia cried, settling in on the floor next to my chair. She was always sitting on the floor or stretching out if she could.

"How is it your fault?" I questioned.

"Um... I don't know, I just feel like it is."

I rolled my eyes as much as I could without wincing. "No, it's my fault. If I hadn't been looking at my—my phone!" I exclaimed, finally remembering why I had lost focus in the car. "Em, run to my room and see if you can find it in my purse!"

She gave me a strange look, but the insistence on my face must have convinced her. She ran away, leaving me alone with Tucker.

He stared at me, and I stared back, remembering that he was on my suspect list, too. He wasn't high ranking, but on there regardless.

I didn't know what to say, and was tired of the runaround, so I blurted out my thoughts. "Is it you? Are you the secret admirer?"

He blinked. Paused. Blinked again. Then burst out laughing. "Me? *Moi*? Your secret admirer? Dang, Spence, haven't we already been down that path?"

I shrugged. "Second chances are a thing."

Tucker wiped at his face, tears forming in his eyes from laughing so hard. "I'm sorry, but that's hysterical. But no, I'm not your secret admirer. How on earth did you even think it was me?"

"Think what was you?" Emilia asked as she rejoined us, handing me my phone. It had a crack on the screen, but was otherwise functional. "And are you allowed to look at this if you have a concussion?"

"She absolutely is not!" Mom called from the kitchen. "Not for a few days at least!"

Emilia plucked the phone out of my hands with her thumb and forefinger, cradling it in her palm as she resumed her position on the floor.

"Spencer thought I was her secret admirer," Tucker answered her earlier question.

Emilia didn't even flinch. "What's on the phone that was so important?" she asked, turning it on and holding it out for me to put my finger to unlock it. Tucker stayed silent, not acknowledging that Em didn't mention anything about him being on the suspect list.

"A clue," I responded, leaning back in my chair. The thought filled me with energy and anxiety at the same time. Would I fail the next challenge too? Would it help with Emilia and Tucker here?

But also... did I care? I had not only lost a round, but also apparently was horrible at figuring out suspects. If I was so bad at it, would I be able to use more clues to help?

Tucker's brows shot up, but once again, he didn't speak. Which was rather unusual for him, but I didn't question it. The ache in my head was getting larger, and all I wanted to do was sleep.

"Hmm..." Em muttered from the floor. "That's odd."

"What?"

"I tried to open the trivia app, but it's not working. It just comes up with an error message and force shuts it down." She turned the phone toward me so I could see it in action for a quick moment.

"I don't know. Maybe something happened to my phone."

She shook her head. "No, everything else is working fine. Just that."

I sighed, really wanting to go back to bed for a nap before my foot appointment. "Guys, I'm sorry, but I'm tired. Thanks for coming to check on me. And for the flowers." I gestured to the bouquet and went to stand.

Tucker stood, sliding one arm under my shoulder and around my back for support. I was too tired to argue.

"Oh, that's not from us. We found it on your doorstep. Let me tell you, when word spread about your accident, it spread fast," Emilia chimed in.

I paused in the doorway, Tucker still around my side. "Wait, *how* did people hear?"

Tucker snorted. "You forget you're student body president. Everyone knows you. You weren't even that far away from the beach. People drove by. People saw. People talk."

"And that's all we knew until now," Emilia added. "That's why we came over. We didn't even know if you would be home from the hospital or not, but took a shot."

"And the flowers weren't from you? Then who?" I asked, turning to look at them. Standing was taking a lot out of me, but I had to know.

Emilia leaned over the table and plucked an envelope out from between the stems. It had been tucked in there so low, I hadn't noticed it before.

But it wasn't any envelope. It was a teal envelope.

Tucker waved his free hand for it, and Em gave it up, a sad smile on her face. "I'll let Tuck get you to bed while I say hi to your mom. Don't read it now, okay? Get some rest."

After Tucker got me to my room, I climbed into bed and watched as he put the envelope on my desk, as far away from me as possible. He winked, said goodbye, and left.

I was back asleep before my head even hit the pillow.

hen I awoke, it was dark. Which it shouldn't have been. I meant to only take a nap before the foot doctor appointment, not sleep all night.

I sat up and immediately regretted it. My head pounded, even though I had enough sleep. I reached over and felt blindly around my nightstand where my phone should have been so I could check the time, but there was nothing there.

We didn't bring upstairs my phone after Emilia checked it for me. So instead, I leaned over, stretching to the back of the cluttered nightstand I planned on cleaning after getting back from the boat, and found my digital clock.

Five forty-two. In the *morning*. I had slept for over twelve hours again. This concussion was giving me more sleep in a day than I had in the past week. Normally, I functioned on maybe six hours a night.

I laid back down, now wide awake. It concerned me that Mom didn't wake me for the appointment, but I supposed sleep was a better way for my body to heal. Knowing her, she rang up the doctor's office as soon as I got to my room and rescheduled. Bless her organizational heart.

After willing myself back to sleep and failing, I sat up again and looked around my room. The glow from the streetlight outside provided a dim illumination across the far side, including on my desk.

Tossing off the covers I didn't remember putting over me, I stumbled to the desk and grabbed the teal envelope.

But nature called first. I went to the bathroom and flipped on the light out of habit and once again regretted it. I switched it off just as quick and felt my way to the toilet. Not only did my headache, but now I had to rewire my brain to *not* do normal daily activities like turn on lights or look at screens.

After I finished, I crawled back into bed. My comforter knocked something on the nightstand over and it made a rattling noise.

Flipping onto my stomach, I leaned down and grabbed it. A bottle of ibuprofen, most likely left there by Mom. Swiping my water bottle, I swallowed two and nestled into my pillows with the teal envelope in hand.

Dear Spencer—

Words cannot portray the guilt racking through me at the moment. Though I have no way of confirming your crash was due to my horrific timing, I'll put the blame solely on myself, anyway.

It was easy enough to put two and two together when the word spread. The trivia app uploaded a new game at 7:32pm, and people said you crashed right around then.

If you haven't already seen, I've shut down the app. I cannot, in good faith, keep it running while you are injured or out of commission in any way. I cannot allow it to stay up as a reminder of your accident. There are many other reasons behind my thought process, but the result remains the same—it is down for good.

As of writing this, I don't know the extent of your injuries. I don't know if you're in the hospital or at home. I'm sending this to your house regardless, but I don't even know when you'll see it. I just had to do something.

The future of the game is in limbo. But it should be the least of your worries at the moment. Please, do not be concerned with the game. You did not fail.

Let me repeat that—You. Did. Not. Fail.

If anything, I did. I should have released the entries on a timed schedule, not randomly, whenever they were finished. There are many things I could have done differently, and I will be living with that.

I'm sorry, Spencer. I don't think if I've ever said that to you before, but I am. So incredibly sorry that I caused this pain and suffering you are going through. If there is something I can do to help, just send word.

I'll be in contact soon. In the meantime, rest. Heal. Don't let this game worry you.

I'm so sorry.

—Your Secret Admirer

I froze. He stopped the game. He *stopped* the game? Emilia mentioned the app was down earlier, but it was *intentional*?

It was bad enough that I failed the round the first time. Now I screwed up so badly that I couldn't even get a chance to redeem myself? That's why I had been so focused on the phone before the crash—it was my time to undo the wrongs I did the night before.

But then I crashed. As someone with a stellar driving record, a crash wasn't just a blemish, it was a giant smear.

Mom and Dad hadn't said a word about it, but if I were them, I would be disappointed in me. I made a stupid decision, and now the consequences were piling up.

Crashed car. Broken foot. Concussion. The game. Not to mention my car, which Dad says was at the shop getting a checkup and repairs.

I was probably the first person in the history of Secret Admirers to have it canceled. Sure, some had dropped out before, but had anyone ever had the *guy* take it away? Not to my knowledge.

Chucking the letter off the bed, I turned onto my side and tried to sleep again.

I must have dozed off for a little bit, because when I awoke, Mom was sitting on the edge of the bed with a cup of coffee, stroking my hair back.

"How's the head? The foot?" she whispered. Light streamed in from the window.

"Decent. Is the appointment for today? I really want to get it done and over with." I was so upset with myself. All I wanted was for the summer to fly by so I could get back to normal.

Mom nodded, handing me the coffee after I sat up. It wasn't quite the same as an order from Sips, but I took what I could get.

"It is. In a few hours, so you have time to wake up and take a shower if you want. Keeping that foot out of the water, that is," she said, pointing to the wrap covering my foot. It had to stay on until I saw the doctor. "Actually, if you want me to draw a bath, it may be easier to keep out of the water? I can wash your hair for you."

I shook my head. "No, I'll just prop it on the side of the tub while I shower. You know, work on my core strength while balancing. And I'll wash my hair another time." I mustered up the best smile I could.

Mom left after another minute of small talk, leaving me alone to get ready. It took double the time I normally would have spent, but hobbling around without falling flat on my face was harder than I thought.

"Good news, dear!" Mom exclaimed as we came into the kitchen. Dad took another day off of work today. Well, at least from going into the office—he was currently settled at the dining table with his laptop and briefcase full of papers.

"What's that?" he asked, not tearing his eyes away from the computer. My heart sunk when I thought of how much time off he was taking due to me. Even though he didn't have to be home today, I knew it was because of me. And since I worked at his office now, I knew what deadlines he was pushing toward and the meetings he was skipping.

"Spence only needs a walking boot for four weeks! It's a hairline fracture in a spot that will most likely heal on its own. No full cast or surgery needed." She put up her purse, glancing at me to make sure I was alright.

The boot was clunky and made me walk with a bit of a limp, but it was better than the crutches. I hobbled into the dining room to show it to Dad, who smiled and winked at me.

"Looks comfy. May get one myself."

I laughed, one of the first times in the past few days. "Ten out of ten do *not* recommend, Dad."

"Dear, where did these cupcakes come from?" Mom exclaimed from the kitchen.

Dad's eyes lit up. "Oh! The bakery delivered them while you were out."

My head snapped up, peering around the corner into the kitchen to see what Mom had found.

She entered the dining room with three cupcakes on a plate, placing one in front of each of us. "Looks like your favorite, Spence. Cookies and cream with Oreo frosting."

I stared at the cupcake suspiciously. "Who sent them?"

Dad shrugged. "No idea. The delivery guy just handed me that envelope." He gestured to the table by the front door where a teal envelope laid.

I bolted to my feet, but Mom stopped me with a hand on my arm. "Sit. I'll get it."

She handed it to, and I tore into it, taking out a small piece of paper.

Dear Spencer

Dear Spencer—

I heard you are home and safe. I hope your injuries aren't too bad and that you're getting rest. In the meantime, enjoy the cupcakes. I know they're your favorite.

—Your Secret Admirer (who is still putting the game on pause, so don't read into this)

"So, who sent them?" Dad asked, still working on the laptop.

A small smile crossed my lips. "A friend."

Chapter 13

"I call this meeting to order. I motion to be the first to speak," I said from my bed, resting against my pillows.

Hosting the student council prep meeting over the phone wasn't quite the way I wanted to do things, but I had to work with my current situation. I couldn't drive, and the doctors restricted me to using a screen only when it didn't make my head hurt. Which, only four days after the accident, was still more often than I wished to admit.

So, speakerphone hosting it was.

"I think we can allow that, Madam President. Are you sure you're feeling alright? We can postpone the meeting—"

"I'm fine. Thank you for your concern, Jen," I said sharply. The new junior class president was sweet, but I didn't want everyone assuming I was less than ready.

"That brings me to my first point. I apologize for the nature of this meeting and appreciate the ability to change at the last minute."

Most people mumbled under their breath that it was no problem or they enjoyed the change anyway. All but Marcus.

"Great, now that we got that part out of the way, can we move on? I need to be first on the agenda, since I have to get this senior budget issue locked down as quick as possible," he said.

I sighed, rubbing at the bridge of my nose. "Please, go ahead Marcus."

He cleared his throat and dove into his speech. The points he made were direct, and his research into vendors was on point, so I didn't have any objections.

Actually, everyone seemed to be more prepared for this meeting than any other one before. It was the most concise, to the point, goal-oriented meeting we ever had. We wrapped in less than thirty minutes.

"Wow, everyone. I don't know if it's because we're on the phone or what, but this meeting was great. Very on target. I appreciate you all taking the time to prepare—"

"Yeah, well, we were told—"

"Anyway, it looks like we're good until the start of school, wouldn't you say, Spence?" Marcus said, interrupting the student body treasurer. "We can all go back to enjoying our summers now."

Rolling my eyes, I agreed. "Yes, that's fine. Thank you everyone. Have a great summer and we'll meet the first week of school."

"See ya!" Marcus called, and one by one, the phones died out. I waited until the end to make sure no one stayed on for extra questions.

"Hey, Spencer?" I heard just before I went to hang up.

"Marcus? I thought you were the first to leave?" I sat up in the bed, unable to stop my curiosity.

"Um, well, yeah..." he mumbled. I heard shuffling in the background. "I just wanted to make sure you were okay. Like, really okay."

My brows shot up in surprise. Marcus had never inquired into my wellbeing before. "Just working through a mild concussion and a hairline fracture. Nothing that would hinder my abilities to be acting student body president, if that's what you were thinking."

Did I think Marcus would take any chance he could to grab my presidential spot? Maybe. Although I did think he was more suited to be senior class president, enjoying all the fun activities to plan and all.

"That's good. I mean, not *good*, but I'm glad it's nothing serious."

The line went silent for a moment, where I almost thought he hung up.

"Was there anything else?" I asked quietly.

He paused again. "No, that was it. Have a great summer."

"You too, Marcus. See you at school." He hung up first, leaving me staring at the phone in my hand, wondering what had just happened.

The next few days were as boring as I could imagine. Dad wouldn't let me back to work until the doctor cleared my concussion, and the appointment for that was next week. I had two good days in a row and even managed to watch an entire episode of a show on Netflix before having to take a screen break yesterday.

Besides reading and listening to music and staring into space, there wasn't much else I could do.

"Spence! You have company!" Mom shouted from downstairs.

I wobbled my way down to see who came to visit. "Marley? What are you doing here?"

Her bright blonde hair was pulled into a high pony tail, allowing her blue eyes to pop against her tan skin. The smile on her face stretched from ear to ear, bringing a much-needed ray of sunshine into my house.

"Hiya! I heard you were put up, and just thought you could use some company?" Her question sounded like a question, a statement, and a demand all rolled into one.

Marley "Sunny" Sorenshine was a walking ball of happiness that brightened most people's day, myself included.

"Yes, please!" I said, ushering her into the living room. "I've never been so bored in my life! Great timing."

She perched on the couch, tucking one long leg under her and spreading out her bright white tennis skirt. "Well, I'm glad I could be of assistance! How have you been feeling?"

I leaned against the pillows, propping my booted foot in front of me. Without being asked, Marley grabbed an extra throw pillow and propped up my foot, giving it a gentle pat when she was done.

"Medically, I'm alright. The concussion symptoms are easing every day and the foot is... there," I groaned, pointing to it. "The boot is this season's hottest accessory, if you didn't know."

Marley giggled, a melodic chime reverberating through the room. "I hadn't heard, but I'll take it into account when planning outfits."

"What's up with you? What have you been doing this summer?" Though Marley and I weren't the best of friends, and it was a little odd for her to visit, I took any company I could get. It was also her personality—she was a mother hen, always checking on people in need.

I guess I classified as a person in need this time.

She shrugged, her tight pink crop top moving with her. "Not a whole lot. Just relaxing, mostly."

"Do you play tennis?" I asked, gesturing to her clothes.

She laughed again. "No. I just like to hang out at the country club because the hot guys use the pool there." She stared at me, her bright blue eyes locking onto my own, before we both burst out laughing.

"Not something I'd do, but sounds like a great plan."

Her grin was infectious. "Hey, we can't all have secret admirers..." She winked.

I groaned, throwing an arm over my face. "No, we can't, can we? Not even I can..."

Marley gasped, but didn't say anything. I knew she was waiting for an explanation though. I couldn't drop that truth bomb and not explain.

"After the accident, he called it off. He told me to 'rest and heal' and 'not to worry about the game.' But I'm not just worried about that, I'm upset because I've completely failed at trying to figure out who he is." I moaned.

"Wait... he *quit*?" Marley whispered.

I nodded. "It seems so. He sent a letter with some flowers after I had the accident, stating how he turned off the app he made to give clues and was deciding what to do next. Then he sent some cupcakes and a note that said the game was still on pause. That was a few days ago, and it's been radio silence since."

Marley's eyes narrowed. "How many clues did you have before he stopped?"

I tilted my head and looked at her. "Three. But it's actually what's outside the clues that I've been using to get a list going."

"Context clues," she affirmed, nodding. "Smart."

I sat up, letting my foot fall to the floor gently. "I didn't put the cupcake clue in yet, though."

"The what in what?"

"My spreadsheet, duh."

"Well, what are we waiting for then? Let's go to work!"

kay, so if you look here, this is their likability score. It started with my own opinion on likely they were to be the secret admirer. But once I figured out some actual clues, it changed based on that. The more direct clues they're related to, the higher the score. If it's related to an indirect clue, it holds some weight, but not as much."

Marley stared at the screen. I had to show her how it worked because I knew I wouldn't be able to look at it for too long. If she could ponder over it, then I could at least talk it out with her and she could input data.

"It looks like..." she scrolled her perfectly pink polished nail down the list, "Jeremy and Chase are in the lead, followed closely by Josh, Marcus, and Theo? But why are they all in red?"

"Because I once had Josh and Theo on top of the list. Then I found out Josh has a girlfriend and Theo doesn't even know my name."

Marley tried to hide her smile, but a little smirk broke through. "Okay, what about Marcus? He still rated high, but he's in red too."

I paused. "Because it's *Marcus*."

She frowned and bopped her head from side to side, considering my comment. "Fair. The two of you are always at each other's throats. I don't understand it. But moving on..."

I perched on the edge of my bed, tucking my legs under me. It felt good to have a fun conversation again, not about my current issues.

"So you said cupcakes? What's special about the cupcakes?"

"They were my favorite flavor. But not one you can just buy at the grocery store. Cookies and cream cupcakes with Oreo frosting."

Marley bit her lip. "Who would know that? I mean, seems like a reasonable thing for someone to learn about you?"

I lifted a finger in the air. "Ah, but see, that's just it. I *only* have them on special occasions. They are not every day cupcakes—they are *celebratory* cupcakes."

Her grin lit up the room again. "Let me guess—you had one the night you won student body president?"

I flipped my hair over my shoulder. "Naturally."

"So, who would know you have one when celebrating?"

"Besides my family? It should be next to no one."

Marley's shoulders slumped. "Boo. Here I thought I was going to be able to help you—"

"Spencer! Delivery!"

Marley jumped up before I could. Which was a blessing,

since jumping onto the boot ended with pain. "I'll get it for you! Stay here."

She bolted out of the room before I could argue, her footsteps getting softer as she ran downstairs.

"You'll... never... guess..." she huffed as she came back a moment later, her arms full with a box.

I stared at her, wondering just what was going on.

"Box. Envelope. Read." She plopped the box on the bed and handed me the envelope.

A teal envelope.

"If you don't want to read it out loud, that's totally cool. I can go..." Marley jerked her thumb over her shoulder, a nervous look on her face.

"No, it's fine. Maybe you'll be able to help me figure out a clue after all." I patted a spot next to me. Having someone new to bounce ideas off of would be refreshing, especially since thinking wasn't my strong suit at the moment.

Marley moved the box and sat on the bed, waiting for me to read.

"Dear Spencer. I debated sending this for a while now. Part of me wanted to call the whole thing quits. The guilt that I feel due to your accident consumed my thoughts for a few days. I couldn't forgive myself knowing that I inadvertently caused you injury." Trying to process what I read, I paused. I would never want anyone to feel guilty about something that happened to me, especially when it wasn't his fault. I was in control of the car and it was my bad decision that led to the accident.

Marley placed a hand on my arm gently, guiding my thoughts back to the letter. "He sounds like a decent guy."

I swallowed my thoughts and moved on. "Yeah, he does." Returning to the letter, I continued. "But then I thought about you. You never accept failure. You always finish what you start and work toward it to the best of your ability. Calling off the game would probably make you feel worse. And it would do nothing to ease my own thoughts. So here we are, back at it, but with a twist."

Marley let out a small, excited squeak.

"I gathered these over the past year, and didn't know what to do with them until now. So here is your last official clue. I know that this clue isn't what you should be doing with a concussion, but... well, just open the box."

I looked at Marley and nodded. "Go ahead," I directed, allowing her to open it.

"Oh, isn't that perfect for you," she giggled, tipping the box to show me what was inside.

Books. The box was full of books. They looked used and old, but the titles fascinated me.

1984. The Handmaid's Tale. Fahrenheit 451. To Kill a Mockingbird.

There were others below, but I stopped searching and continued reading. "I don't think you're allowed to read with a concussion, but hopefully soon. Though, I'm sure you've already read a bunch of them."

I stopped and rolled my eyes. Of course I already read a bunch of them.

"There're probably ten or twelve books in this box. No wonder I could barely carry it up the stairs," Marley said, still looking through them.

I read on as she looked. "Anyway, if you want to call off the game, please do. If it's too much for you, just let the neutral party know. Or anyone. Your friends. Someone. They'll get word to me somehow. I'm speeding up the timeline, even if you haven't figured out who I am. I want you to finish the game, just like everyone else. Even if I screwed it all up. You'll find out everything soon. Until then, your secret admirer."

I placed the letter down on the bed and looked toward my computer. A wave of sadness washed over me, and I wasn't sure why. I should have been happy that he kept the game going, even if it was only with one last clue. "Do you mind updating the list?" I asked Marley.

She jumped up and crossed the room to my desk, spinning in the chair to face my laptop. "Who and what?"

"That's the hard part. See, his clues are never straight forward, so I have to go backwards about it." What did all these books have in common? Why would someone give me a box of old books?

"Maybe someone who knows you like books? Someone who collects classics? Or..." she drifted off, biting the end of her nail in thought.

"Right? It's not so easy. But these books..." I lifted one up and stared at it. The spine was cracked, and the cover was slightly faded due to age.

"Wasn't *1984* banned for, like, the longest time?" Marley asked.

My head snapped up to stare at her, causing me to wince. "Yeah. So was this one." I held up *The Handmaid's Tale*.

Looking in the box, I realized they were *all* banned at one time or another. Some still topped the banned books charts in certain places. "That's it, Marley. You're a genius!"

She reached back and flicked her blonde ponytail, smiling. "That's not something I get called often, so I'll take it. Now... *why* am I a genius?"

I pointed to the laptop. "Let's get some new data entered."

"So, you think whoever is your secret admirer had to be in either your US History class, or on the debate team with you?" Marley asked, scrolling down the list, searching.

"Exactly. Banned books are a weeklong discussion in US History, and our first topic for debate last year was banned books. It was the first practice round back in like September, but it matches."

Marley pointed to the list. "Who am I adding? Or are we eliminating?"

"Both. Never rule anyone out."

"You've already ruled out Josh, Theo, Marcus and Connor, though," she pointed out.

I let out a huff. "They're still there. Just... ignored."

She giggled and turned to place her hands over the keyboard. "Ready when you are, Captain!"

"Okay, let's start with US History. Read me the names on the list?"

As she went through one by one, I replied with a simple yes or no. If I said no, she highlighted them in red to eliminate them. There would be no reason why someone would stay if they had no connection to this specific clue.

"Alright, that took out all the swimmers," she stated, clicking the final buttons. "Also, Andrew, Joey, and Max."

She pouted for a moment. "Poor Max. Though if he was your secret admirer and didn't tell me, I'd kill him."

I laughed. "I forgot you guys were best friends! Honestly, he was on the list, but really at the very bottom."

"BFFs since diapers. Our moms are best friends, so it was kind of inevitable. That and being neighbors. Proximity rules all, right?" Her grin was infectious.

"That leaves who?" I questioned.

"That leaves... Chase, Jeremy, Drew, and Davis."

Nodding, I mentally went through the debate team roster from this year. "Take Davis and Drew out. Chase and Jeremy were in debate with me, though."

She did as asked. "Chase, and Jeremy are our top two contenders then. Do I need to up their likability score or anything? Or put the reasoning?"

I instructed her on how to update the rest of the sheet and within a few minutes, everything was done.

"It looks like Chase is slightly above the rest—" Marley started, just as her phone rang.

She apologized and answered it, taking quietly and quickly to whoever was on the other end. "I'm sorry, I have to go. I forgot Max and I were headed to the beach."

Before she made it to the door, she looked back. "That was so rude of me. I'm sorry, do you want to come to the beach with us? There's always room for more!"

I smiled, but shook my head. "No, that's alright. Tell Max I say hi and that he's officially off the list. I think I'm going to take a nap. Thank you so much for coming to visit and helping with the clues!"

She grinned and crossed the room to give me a hug. "Thanks for letting me help! I'm glad to see you're feeling better. Maybe when you're up for it, we can go grab some ice cream."

It took another day at home before Mom let me out of the house. By then, I was so deprived of the outside world, I forgot what it was like to be normal. Other than doctor's appointments, I hadn't been anywhere since the accident. And doctors didn't quite count as social interaction.

Today, Mom was taking me to get my hair done. I hadn't had it cut in about six months, since I was busy with campaigning and the end of the school year, so she wanted to treat me.

What I really wanted to do was hit the beach with my friends again, but I appreciated her offer. I never minded spending extra time with Mom; we were so alike, it was like being around a friend anyway.

"You look gorgeous, Spence. Really, I think the layers were a fabulous idea, and the bangs? Wow! I never would have thought about it for you, but the way they just barely brush the top of your glasses makes you look so much older and sophisticated," Mom said as we pulled out of the parking lot.

I fluffed the bangs, still unsure about them myself. But if Mom said they looked good, then they probably did. She would never compliment something she didn't truly believe was worth it. Bangs were a spur-of-the-moment decision. My stylist mentioned it once, and the thought sat in my mind all through the shampoo and trim. I went in wanting a change, and I definitely got one.

"Want to swing by Sips on the way back?" Mom asked. My venture into freedom had been limited, so I would take any extra time I got.

"Absolutely," I said without hesitation. A thought sparked as she mentioned the coffee shop downtown. Jeremy's family owned it. And every now and then, when they were in a bind or short staffed, he would step up and work behind the counter.

Jeremy was more like me, on the nerdy side, so being a barista wasn't his strong suit. He did love coming up with new coffee combinations, which usually got pawned off on willing students when he got to school in the morning, but serving was more of an anxiety inducing job. It definitely wasn't for me, either.

But considering Jeremy was in the top two on my list, and the only person I had yet to see in person since this game started, getting coffee sounded like a great plan to me.

The only problem with the plan was the fact that Mom pulled into the drive through, and didn't park so we could go inside.

"Your foot, sweetheart," she said when I questioned her about it. "I figured you'd rather keep it rested than walk around with the boot?" The sad frown on her face was like a knife to my heart. All she wanted was to do what was best for me, so who was I to argue?

I gave her a smile and agreed with her. It was cumbersome to walk around with the boot on, and her heart was in the right place.

"One large cold brew, and one salted caramel, dark chocolate mocha, extra hot, no whip, please!" Mom said loudly through the drive through speaker.

The voice crackled on the other side. "Your total is eight seventy-five—wait, is this Spencer?"

I perked up. It had to be Jeremy on the other side. "Jeremy?" I shouted, leaning across the car and Mom.

"Yeah, hi! Hey I heard—sorry, yes, I know—" he cut off for a moment, as he was obviously talking to someone in the building and not to us anymore.

"Your total is eight seventy-five, please pull up to the window," he said a moment later.

Mom stared at me, but I just shrugged. I had no idea what that was about either.

A second later, we were at the window, Jeremy's face smiling at us with his headset moved aside so he could speak.

"Hey! I thought that was you. Not every day we get that specific order, especially since it's not a menu item. Haven't had anyone order it in a few weeks, but I remembered it because it sounds so good. I heard you were in an accident, though. Are you alright?" He handed Mom her cold brew and she handed him her credit card.

I leaned over her again. "Yes, I'm fine. I had a concussion and a hairline fracture in my foot, but it's no big deal." I glared at Mom before she could argue.

"Wow, I'm so sorry to hear you were hurt." Jeremy reached out and handed me my coffee order. "I was out of town last week, or else I would have messaged you or something sooner. Just got back yesterday."

"Oh, no worries," I said, returning to my seat. "Hope to see you over the summer!"

Mom pulled away, but remained silent, which gave me time to sip my coffee and ponder. All while my brain went haywire, knowing another name was taken off the list and it was down to one.

*A*fter our excursion, Mom dropped me off at home so she could go visit Grandma. She offered to take me with her, but I needed to do some thinking.

Opening my laptop, I scrolled through the list, putting Jeremy in red among the others.

He had been out of town all last week, only coming back yesterday. Which meant he hadn't even heard of my accident until yesterday. Which meant he couldn't have sent the flowers, cupcakes, or books.

So it was Chase. I mentally kicked myself for not paying more attention to him while we were at the festival. But I had been so dead-set on it being Theo, that I hadn't really given Chase much thought. At that point, Tucker was also on the list, and I didn't think about him at all either.

I tried to replay some of the moments of that day, but I couldn't recall everything. I remembered seeing Theo, his burps, his abs, and the nonsense about not knowing who I was, but the further into the evening, the fuzzier my memory got. The doctors said it was normal, especially the closer I got to the accident, because of the concussion, but it was still frustrating.

It didn't matter anyway. Everything pointed to Chase McNeill being my secret admirer. The only problem was that I wasn't sure how I felt about it.

I liked Chase. We had a lot in common, were great study partners, and he was a great guy. But... I never thought of him in any other way. Actually, I always pictured him with someone else.

My phone buzzed with a message, but I ignored it. Ever since the app went down, I didn't react to my phone the same way I had earlier in the month. Messages could wait a few minutes to get to now.

But when it buzzed again, my interest piqued. Even more so when it went off another time. Three more buzzes came through before I could cross the room to grab it.

> **MYA:** Spencer, what's going on? What am I missing?

> **EMILIA:** Girl, you need to check this out. When did you plan this?

> **SKYE:** SPENCER! Totes not fair that you're throwing a party without me! You couldn't wait??

> **TUCKER:** Um... what? I want in.

> **MYA:** Seriously, Spence, what is going on? I feel so out of the loop!

> **CHASE:** Private event? And I wasn't invited? Rude.

I blinked a few times, my brain trying to process all their messages at once. I had no idea what they were talking about, so I threw them all into one group chat to get to the bottom of this.

> **ME:** What are all of you going on about?

> **SKYE:** You haven't seen?

> **EMILIA:** It's all over Instagram

> **MYA:** Honestly, if I keep finding out things because of Instagram or TikTok and not from you guys personally, I'm going to be upset.

> **ME:** Guys... I'm confused.

> **TUCKER:** Check. Your. Insta. Duh.

I clicked out of the message and opened the app. The first post on my feed didn't seem all that out of place.

But the next one was. And the one after that. The more I scrolled, the more I saw.

Multiple people posted the exact same photo, seemingly at the exact same time.

I zoomed in on one of them, posted by... Josh? What in the crazy multiverse was going on?

The picture was of a campaign poster. With *my* face.

"Um... what?" I whispered, still scrolling and finding more and more of the same post. "What is going on?"

I took a screenshot and returned to the group message.

> **ME:** Is this what you are all going crazy about?

> **MYA:** Yes! It's everywhere! You already won though, so what is this?

> **EMILIA:** Yeah, as your unofficial campaign manager, why wasn't I aware of this event?

CHASE: More importantly, why wasn't I invited?

ME: It's not me, guys. I have no idea what this is...

TUCKER: Then who did it?

My mind spun. Who did it definitely was the question. Who would post multiple posters with my face on it, and why?

ME: There's only one thing I can think of...

SKYE: YOUR SECRET ADMIRER!

EMILIA: Didn't he quit?

ME: No...

I left it open, seeing if Chase would jump in there. If he was behind this, would he give himself away?

TUCKER: The 20th is tomorrow. Do you think you're supposed to go? Does private mean just you and him?

CHASE: I ask again, why wasn't I invited??? Doesn't your secret admirer know that we're all like a package deal? Where Spencer goes, we all go?

There it was. Either Chase was trying to cover his tracks or... he *wasn't* my secret admirer. And if he wasn't, then who was?

> **ME:** I'll figure it out. I need to reevaluate things.

> **MYA:** If you need help, just text me!

> **EMILIA:** Want me to come over and look things over with you?

> **TUCKER:** I'll start walking over now!

> **ME:** No, it's fine. Let me do some thinking. I'll let you all know.

I put my phone down, racking my brain trying to think of what this meant. Whoever made this is planning something for tomorrow. Maybe it's some sort of victory party? A private event in my honor? I never really celebrated winning student body president, outside the normal celebratory dinner at home and my special cupcakes...

On the other hand, it could be someone trying to overthrow me. Or a prank—someone hoping I'll show up so they can humiliate me.

One name jumped into my mind as I thought that. Marcus. Would he would really do that, though? He got senior class president. It's not like he didn't win something. And why sabotage me weeks after winning, during the summer, when we weren't even in school?

I rubbed my temples, a headache starting to come on. We've always been at each other's throats, flip flopping between presidencies— I froze as a flood of information rushed through me. All the blood drained from my face as realization hit.

I leaped off my bed, falling into my desk chair so fast it slid across the floor. I had to scooch myself back to my desk ungracefully, where I finally opened my laptop, waiting impatiently while it started up.

As soon as the screen flickered to life, I opened the spreadsheet with the list of suspects.

"I was wrong," I muttered to myself, peering at the screen.

Dragging the cursor over Marcus' name, I clicked into the box under reasoning, and began typing.

I discounted him after the early decision clue, not adding anything else to his box. Now, I had to add the last few clues to his name—US History. Debate. Cupcakes. Coffee. Poster.

Marcus was indeed in my US History class, but that wasn't as important as debate. He had been my opponent on banned books. He had been in favor of banning, while I countered against him.

Just like every election we went up against each other in.

Just like every election that I won and had cookies and cream cupcakes with Oreo frosting as a celebration. Like the time Mom had them sent to school for the first student council meeting after I won freshman year.

Who could make a campaign poster look exactly like a real one? Someone who had experience making them, of course.

And who was the last one that ordered my favorite coffee from Sips a few weeks ago? Marcus, the last day of school, before the Transfer.

I let out a huge breath, all the air in my lungs escaping as I leaned back into my chair, running my hands through my hair. Pulling at the strands, I chastised myself for not seeing it sooner.

After I pulled up the original trivia app clues, I pieced things together even more.

"Clue one," I whispered to myself. Saying it out loud made it seem more real. And also made me feel stupider than before. "Closer than you may think, yet so far away. In the shadows I've always been, but now I'm ready to play."

I tapped my fingers on the desk, creating a beat to my thoughts. "Closer than you may think..." Marcus had always been right by my side through the years. Whether on council seats, debate team, beside me in every election, he was there. The years I beat him for president, he would have been in my shadow. Especially now, when I got the student body president over him. But he had the senior class seat. Did that mean he was ready to play? Or did he mean the secret admirer game?

"Clue two. More flip flops than a beach in summer." It dawned on me. Flip-flops? Not the shoe, but the change in our presidencies, the back and forth for debate, our usual sassy banter.

"Wow. If this month was meant to make me feel dumb, then at least that was a success." I dropped my head into my hands as a knock came at my door.

The app. The SAT words. The early decision. All led to Marcus—one of the smartest, but slyest, guys at Ryder High.

And someone I assumed hated me more than liked me. Someone I never looked twice at because of that assumption. But also, someone who pushed me. Who kept me grounded and humble. Who forced me to do my best, if only to compete against him.

"Spence? You hungry yet?" Mom asked, poking her head in.

I sighed. "No. Mom, what do you do when you feel like an idiot?"

She frowned and gestured to the bed. I nodded, and she perched on the edge, her hands clasped in her lap. "Well, sweetheart, I think it would depend on the context. Why do you feel like an idiot? You are the smartest girl I know, after all."

A small huff of a laugh escaped me. "Thanks, Mom. But what if..." I struggled on how to phrase this without having to explain the entire Secret Admirer thing. "What if you mistakenly left someone out of something, only to realize later that it was them the whole time, and you missed all the hints?"

She grinned. "Does this have anything to do with a teal envelope earlier this month and the deliveries as of late?"

I nodded, hanging my head. "Yeah."

"Is the messenger anyone I know?"

The internal struggle went back and forth. Did I openly admit that it was Marcus, and everything I thought about the two of us had been wrong?

"I think... he likes me," I said, staring at my hands.

"Who?"

I covered my face with my fingers, peeking out between them. "Marcus Edmond."

The smile on her face grew wider. "I always liked that kid."

"Are we talking about the same Marcus?"

Mom nodded and stood to leave. "Yup. Every time you lost to him, you were reminded that someone else could do the job just as well. He taught you that if it couldn't be you, it could still be done. Some may see that as a horrible lesson to learn, but you had to learn not to control everything. The hard way. you had to relinquish control to someone you didn't like, live with it, and then pick up and try again. He pushed you to be better, to make good choices, and run your campaigns for the better of the student body, instead of only against him. He taught you humility with grace."

My face scrunched up in confusion. How had Mom figure all that out and I hadn't?

"He pushed her to the point where she thought she hated him, only to realize that it wasn't hatred, it was a delicate balance between healthy competition and striving to be better for him. For herself," I whispered to myself.

Mom stopped in the doorway. "I have no idea what you mean, but that kind of sums up the two of you. Always going against each other, not realizing that if you worked together, you two would be a massive force to be reckoned with. Snacks are downstairs, and dinner will be ready in just over an hour."

My entire body felt like someone drenched me with ice water.

Chapter 17

"I cannot believe you chose me to escort you to your funeral," Tucker said.

Truthfully, neither could I. I needed a friend to come with me, per Mom's rules for leaving the house with a broken foot and post-concussion. But why I chose Tucker, I wasn't sure. I needed someone who would be there in case this whole thing went sideways and I left in a ball of tears.

"First of all, don't call it my funeral. He's supposed to be my secret admirer," I chastised, smacking him in the chest. He was driving my car since he didn't have one, and I couldn't drive yet with the boot. "And second, hit me with the reasons I should like him back. Because most of my high school years I've spent thinking he hated me, so it's going to take a little bit to change this mindset."

Tucker nodded, his face growing serious. "Understandable. But you realize he's never hated you, right? Most of us have known that for a while. He's admired you for years, Spence. Always going against you, even though he knows he'll lose most of the time. He even stayed on the debate team just because of you. Because he liked arguing with you and watching you get all worked up. Sure, he pushes your buttons, but he does so *because* he likes you."

"That's some backwards thinking there. Like telling a little girl that the boy who chased her around the playground likes her," I said.

"Exactly. Well, in that case, the girl should clearly state her boundaries, but in this case, you've done that. You and Marcus have been side by side for years. It's a healthy push-and-pull relationship. Think back to Transfer."

We pulled into the parking lot of the address listed on the campaign poster. As Tucker put the car in park, I thought about the last day of school.

"As senior class president, he had the right to lead the class into the courtyard," I started, not seeing what Tucker meant.

"He did," Tuck agreed. "But what did he do instead?"

I paused, remembering the emptiness I felt when I saw him run to the front of the group to lead everyone out. And the utter shock that came when he reached back for me, to take the charge with him. Side by side.

"He even had my favorite coffee," I mumbled, as more lightbulbs went off.

"He never got me coffee, and I was the treasurer sophomore year when he was president," Tucker exclaimed.

Thinking back, Marcus hadn't just gotten me coffee that one time. He brought me something almost every student council meeting. And each year, at the biggest debate tournament, he always remembered to sneak a bag of Skittles into my briefcase. It had become a tradition; one I didn't put too much thought into until now.

"Wow. I really missed all the clues, didn't I?" I leaned my head against the car window, wondering just how I could have been so oblivious.

Tucker laughed. "When you make a decision on something, you tend to get your head stuck in the sand, so to say. Could be why you and I didn't work out…"

I backhanded him in the chest again, but lightly. "That's not why, but whatever."

Tucker glanced at his watch. "It's almost time. Are you going to go in?"

Looking out the window, I stared at the front door of a place I knew rather well. The bowling alley is where Marcus held his "campaign rallies" every year. He always said it was because his cousin owned it, so it was free, but it was more because they could also party after the results came in.

"We're sure it's not a prank?" I asked, turning back to Tucker. My gut reaction was to expect a pie in the face, or silly string covering me the second I walked into that building. I couldn't wrap my mind around the fact that Marcus Edmond was my secret admirer. That he somehow went all this time liking me when I thought he hated me.

Tucker laughed. "I don't think it's a prank. I promise, if I did, I wouldn't let you go in there."

I nodded slowly, undoing my seatbelt and making sure the straps on my boot were tight. "Well, I guess it's now or never."

With one hand on the door handle, I hesitated, trying to gather my composure, just like I did before every big event or speech.

"Spence?" Tucker called just as I swung my legs onto the pavement. "Go easy on him, okay? He's probably more nervous than ever before."

I tilted my head in confusion. "Why would you say that?"

"Because telling a girl you like her, or asking someone out for the first time, is a way more nerve wracking than running for class president. It's personal."

My heart pounded. He was right, of course. As much as I have been nervous in my life before campaigns or debates, this feeling inside was completely different. I swallowed the lump in my throat, my palms clammy. "Okay."

"Okay. Go slay, queen," he said with a smile as I got to my feet and closed the door. Glancing back, I found Tucker reclining the driver's seat and opening a book. I hadn't asked him to wait for me, but it looked like he was, anyway.

Before entered through the front doors, I sucked in another breath, holding it in my chest for a count of five, and letting it go as slowly as possible in an attempt to calm my racing heart.

It took a moment for my eyes to adjust to the darkness of the bowling alley. It was completely empty.

My mind raced as I stepped further inside, not seeing anyone, even employees. Did I have the wrong day? The wrong time? Was this actually a prank like I expected?

After a few more steps, I came to the nearest table and leaned against it, taking the weight off my foot. I was about to pull my phone out of my back pocket when someone interrupted me.

"Does it hurt?"

I whirled around, finding Marcus behind me, his hands stuffed into the pockets of his khaki shorts and a frown on his face. He had his glasses on today, instead of the new contacts he had gotten a few weeks ago.

"What?" I whispered, pushing my own glasses higher on my face. Marcus stopped a few feet away, staring down at his shoes.

"Your foot. Does it hurt?" His voice was so soft, I almost didn't hear him. This wasn't the normal Marcus I was used to. He was usually loud, ready to rally the troops, to make his voice heard. I don't think I've ever heard him whisper before.

I glanced down at my boot. "A little, sometimes. If I walk too much on it. But it's not that bad. The boot is just to give it structure, so it heals correctly. It should be off in the next few weeks."

He nodded and finally started toward me again, his eyes now locking on mine. I held his gaze, uncertain what was going to happen. I didn't want to be the one to start, as I still wasn't sure what was going on.

"Spence, I..." he started, stopping before he got too close. He was within arm's reach, but felt so far away. The Marcus in front of me wasn't the Marcus I knew. This Marcus was different. He was nervous, shy, uncertain.

"This isn't a prank, is it?" I blurted out. I had no idea why I was so certain that none of this was real, but I couldn't get it off my mind.

The smile I knew so well filled his face. "No. No, this isn't a prank. I would never do that to you."

"Why's that so funny?" I questioned, my tone becoming more defensive than I meant to. Tucker warned me to go easy on him, and I already failed.

Marcus shook his head and took a step forward. "Because it's so typically *you*, Spence. You are your own protector, never letting anyone chip at your armor. That brick wall you've built over your heart cannot be broken until *you* decide to let it. Trust me, I've spent years trying."

My face fell. "What? Years? Marcus, I... I thought... I thought you hated me this whole time."

"Never. In fact, the moment you beat me for class president freshman year is the moment I realized how much I liked you. Remember what you did when we found out the results?"

I pondered for a moment while lowering myself into the chair behind me. Marcus joined me at the table, in the seat across from me.

"I... I'm not sure, actually. It was a long time ago."

The smile on his face softened. "You walked right up to me, held out your hand, and said 'Great campaign. You worked hard and had some outstanding positions on your platforms. I hope we can take this as a learning experience and I look forward to future races.'"

That got a laugh out of me. "I sound stuck up and pretentious."

He shook his head, a few strands of blonde hair falling over his face. During school, he had it perfectly combed back and glued in place with product. His whole look was always tailored, from his collared polos to his shoes.

But summer Marcus was more laid back and relaxed. From gym shoes to shorts, t-shirts and messy hair, summer Marcus was almost... hot? Not that the Marcus I saw wasn't attractive, I just never thought about him in that manner. But staring at him now... I never realized how cute he really was. He was exactly the type of guy I normally went for, yet had always written him off.

"You weren't pretentious. You were confident. You've always been your own best ally, making sure that even in times of loss you composed yourself. When I won sophomore year, you were the first to congratulate me and offer your support. You shot down anyone who said you should have won over me. You stood beside me the entire year, never saying how you would have done something better or gave me unsolicited advice."

The look in his eyes told me he wasn't lying. He truly admired me over the years, and I never saw it. I only caught the smirks or the sarcasm and made assumptions.

"I'm so sorry, Marcus," I whispered. "All this time... but why now? Why this?"

MARCUS

I pursed my lips, hesitating a moment. "I couldn't do it during the school year. I don't think I would have been able to handle seeing you attempt to figure out who I was in person. And if you rejected me in the end? If you didn't show? Well.."

Spencer's bright green eyes shone behind her tortoiseshell glasses, staring at me with expectation.

"I've always known what you thought of me, Spencer. And to some degree, I played it up. The rest of the student body pinned us against each other for years, and that's the role we had to play. Rivals. Enemies. Opponents. But that has *never* been the way I've seen you. And you've never treated me as such either. You've always had class, always rose above defeat to be the better person. To everyone else, we have always been on opposite sides, but if you look closer... we've never been more alike."

The small quiver in my voice was unexpected and didn't go unnoticed by her. Her eyebrows raised before a serious look crossed her face as she dove into deep thought.

For once, I stayed silent. I wanted her to figure out exactly what I meant without me having to spell it out. I knew she knew. She's always known, I just never pointed it out. In fact, I actively tried to hide our similarities behind sarcasm or misdirection.

"Humility with grace," she whispered, staring down at the table. Her glasses slipped down her nose slightly, and her hair fell around her like a curtain.

Reaching an arm out, I pushed the hair back on one side, tucking it behind her ear. "What's humility with grace?" I said softly.

She stared at me, quiet for a moment. Just when I didn't think she was going to answer, she spoke. "What my mom said. She said you taught me humility with grace over the years. Learning to lose the right way and still power on. She said that by you winning, it taught me how to lose control and be alright with it."

I grinned. "Well, that's true. You do like to be in control."

Spencer shook her head, lifting it more and squaring her shoulders. Her confidence was returning and power Spencer was back.

"I do. But I also admit when I am wrong and admit defeat."

I held up a hand to stop her. "This isn't defeat, Spencer. You didn't lose anything."

She tucked her lips in for a moment. "Yes, I did. I took you off my suspect list way too early in this game.

I discounted you due to my blindness and inability to recognize qualities that have been there since the start of our working relationship."

My heart dropped to the floor. Power Spencer turned into President Spencer so fast, I missed the transition. Instead of breaking that brick wall, she was adding to it, as if I was another conquest she lost.

"Cut the crap, Spencer," I said as boldly as I dared. I leaned back in the chair, folding my arms over my chest and raising an eyebrow, daring her to call me out.

"Excuse me?"

I jutted my chin in her direction, putting on the same show she decided to. "You heard me. Cut the crap. You know that little speech you just gave me was bull."

She huffed, drawing back as if I slapped her. "It most certainly was not—"

"Spencer."

She paused. Her bottom lip quivered just once, but I saw it.

"Like I said. I've known my feelings for you since freshman year. Almost three years I've been holding back on you. And know what I've learned about you in almost three years?" This time I sat forward, my elbows on the table, my hands clasped together, staring her down.

The lip trembled again, and she quickly tucked it in before shaking her head no.

"In almost three years, I not only know your favorite coffee order, but your favorite breakfast muffin from the cafeteria. I know that you always like to take a seat in the front row, but by the door, not the windows, so you don't get distracted during class. I know that you will routinely skip lunch to help tutor a friend, even if it's in a class you don't take. I know your favorite way to celebrate your victories is with your favorite—"

"Cupcake," she finished for me.

I nodded. "It's not quite the same as the parties I've thrown here for my wins, but yeah. You celebrate with a cupcake. I also know how hurt you get when you lose, or when you think something is taken from you. I know how much it pained you to see me lead the Transfer, when you hoped it would be you on that bench."

Her face crumpled. "That's why you—"

"That's why I took you with me. I brought you coffee in hopes it would soften the blow, and had you right by my side because that's where you *belong*, Spencer." I paused, thinking about how I worded that. "No, that's not right. *I* belong by *your* side. That's where I've always been. That's where I hope to stay."

Her mouth flapped open and closed as she gathered her thoughts. Before she could get anything out, I butted in one last time.

"And one more thing—if this doesn't work out, if you don't want anything to happen between us, you still have my full and utter support in everything. I will always stand by your side and champion you. Just like I've always done, I will continue to do. You have my word on that."

That was it. That was all I had to say. I hadn't planned on half of it, but it was right. The ball was in her court.

Or, as it seemed, her alley.

"Should we bowl for it?" she asked, a wicked gleam sparkling in her eye.

That took me by surprise. "What?"

Spencer popped to her feet, as gracefully as she could with the boot on, and extended her hand toward me. "If we're always competing against each other for everything else, why not this? Let's bowl for it."

It only took me a millisecond to agree to that. I leaped up, ran to the back, turned on the lane closest to us, and grabbed two balls from the racks, bringing them to the front.

"I get some leeway because of the foot," she declared as she stuck her fingers into her ball.

I shook my head. "No argument there, Madam President. Can I add one stipulation to the agreement, though?"

She paused, then nodded. "You may."

"If I win... can I kiss you?"

Her eyes grew wide and her smile dropped. But only for a moment, before her face softened. "I'll allow it."

My brows shot up so fast. "Wow, that was a quick agreement. Why so fast?"

She hobbled toward the lane, swung the ball back, and let it fly down the alley. She knocked down seven pins on the first throw. "Because I don't plan on losing, obviously."

Ten frames later, there was a sore loser on the bench.

"You're cute when you pout," I said, settling next to her.

She stuck her tongue out at me. After a moment of silence, she spoke. "Just so you know, I wasn't really playing for keeps."

That got my complete attention. "You weren't? I thought..."

She sat up and turned toward me. "You thought that if I won, I would leave and not give us a shot. And that if you won, you not only got a new girlfriend, but that kiss you wagered."

I nodded, as that was exactly what I assumed "Let's bowl for it" meant.

"Well, it's not. Either way, I wasn't going to back down from a challenge. Do you even know me?"

That got the biggest chuckle out of me. I wrapped an arm around the back of the bench behind her. "Spence, I know you almost better than you know yourself. Why do you think I took you up on this challenge so fast?"

She looked at me, questioning.

"Because I know you're horrible at bowling, even without the boot. It was a for sure victory. Hence the reason I added the stipulation." I threw a wink in her direction, causing her to roll her eyes.

"I see. So you went into this knowing you would win, and even though I wasn't playing for what you thought I was, you still did it. You are that certain that we would be good together?"

To her dismay, I bopped her on the nose. "I've been certain for almost three years. Just too chicken to do anything about it until now."

She nodded, still biting her bottom lip. "Well, a bet is a bet, and I admit defeat. Congratulations, Mr. Senior Class President, you have yourself a new girlfriend."

Spencer stood, balancing more on her good leg than her bad. I jumped to my feet, standing only about an inch or so taller than her. "I believe there was a condition on the bet."

She locked eyes with me and a small smile crossed her lips. She lifted her hands, resting them on my shoulders. "There was. And I always pay up."

Leaning over, she pressed her lips to mine for what felt like a millisecond and an eternity at the same time. All I knew was that it was everything I had been waiting for, and entirely too short.

"I'm going to need to start making more bets," I whispered into her ear before she pulled away.

"And I—oh no!" she exclaimed, her hands flying to her cheeks and her eyes wide with fear. "Tucker!"

My brows furrowed in confusion. "Tucker? What about Tucker?"

"He's still in the car!"

Want more Spencer and Marcus?
Grab a bonus scene by visiting
https://bit.ly/dearspencerbonusscene
and see what happens before the game
began and Marcus was creating his app!

Did you love *Dear Spencer*? I'd love to hear!
Drop a review for me on Amazon and
let me know your thoughts!

Keep reading the *Love Notes* series.
Available on Amazon.

Looking for another supersmart girl trope story? How about fake dating and revenge plots mixed in? Check out *Imperfections in the Plan* today!

When Robin creates the perfect plan for revenge, will it work against her high school bully?

The once methodical world around sixteen-year-old Robin Engelbretson has taken a tumultuous turn.

She's known as the science nerd, and doesn't mind the label one bit. Spending her time studying and doing homework, Robin's never been one for a big social life, unlike her sister Hazel.

Tired of having her own twin sister be her biggest bully, Robin devises a plan to bring her down and give her a taste of what it's like at the bottom of the high school hierarchy.

Step one- making Hazel jealous by getting her ex-boy-friend to agree to be her fake-boyfriend. But Hazel is a master of manipulation, and steps two through five may be harder than Robin anticipated.

Robin will do anything to make sure her plan succeeds, but at what cost?

Will Robin lose sight of everything important to her, or can she catch herself before she falls too deep into the world of revenge?

Read *Imperfections in the Plan* today!

ACKNOWLEDGEMENTS

We finally have our first repeat girl! But don't worry, we introduced more characters too. Are you keeping track of everyone?? Any and all names are eligible to appear again, so keep an eye out!

I cannot thank you all enough for loving on these books! Every review you leave, every message you send, every time you share with your friends, it warms my heart and makes me so, so happy!

To the people who keep me moving and motivated every day, Shain and Andrea, thank you my friendsss! You badass author gals are my favs!

My alpha and beta readers who indulge me every month when I send them random things, and don't hate me when I tell them I changed massive chunks over and over—Tara, Cristina, Robynne, Stephanie, and Andrea— you guys rock!

To Amanda, who grabbed the book, sped read, and gave me feedback when I needed a quick run through but couldn't physically look at it myself anymore. I totally named that EMT after you! 100% no lie.

Danielle Keil

To Stephanie, the most amazing cover designer/formatter/ friend extraordinaire—you are also my fav and this series (ahem- all my books) wouldn't be anything without you!

My Dandelions, my booktokers, my IG friends and beyond—thank you all for grabbing this series and running with it. A series made on a whim turned out to be one of the best decisions of my career thus far, and you are all to thank!!

ABOUT THE
Author

Danielle Keil grew up in the Chicagoland area. A recent transplant, she is enjoying the Mississippi life, especially the pool in her backyard.

Danielle has been happily married for over 10 years, and has two young children, a daughter and a son, who are exact replicas of her and her husband.

Danielle's love language is gifts, her Ennegram is a 9w1, and she loves everything purple.

The way to her heart is through coffee, chocolate and tacos (extra guac).

Want to hang out?
Find her on Facebook, Instagram, and TikTok!

Learn more at
authordaniellekeil.com

Made in the USA
Coppell, TX
07 September 2022

82794495R00090